TORNADO
SEASON

TORNADO SEASON

COURTNEY CRAGGETT

Black
Lawrence
Press

Black
Lawrence
Press

www.blacklawrence.com

Executive Editor: Diane Goettel
Chapbook Editor: Kit Frick
Book Design: Amy Freels
Cover Design: Zoe Norvell

Published 2019 by Black Lawrence Press.
Printed in the United States.

For Cara, Kelsey, and Kylee

CONTENTS

KANSAS BEFORE OZ

When we were very young the world spun with colors that other people did not see. It began in the nursery. You cried and your tears filled the room with a bruised sunset. I covered my ears at the parade we watched because the orange of the blaring trumpets was too bright. And at bedtime we fell asleep to the deep, midnight blue of the night train that drove through town. "Do you see it too?" I whispered with my hand in yours, and you nodded and we knew that we were not alone.

You were not my brother, but we were children together. Nobody told us why, and we did not need to know. Our mother tucked us in and sang prayers to us with her voice of silvery purple, and we hugged her goodnight and breathed in her hues.

I did not know that my colors belonged to you. We had just graduated from high school when the tornado hit our house. It stole you from me, and you stole the colors. The doctors said I hit my head. They said that perhaps my hearing was damaged and that my ears would ring forever. They asked me if it hurt, and I nodded and said it is a knife. But I did not say that it took away the colors, that now the world no longer spins but is still and gray. They brought me into a booth and hooked wires to my ears and played sounds for me. "Can you hear it?" they asked me. I said yes, I can hear it. But I cannot see it, I thought.

When we were children, you called my name one night and together we slipped out of our bedroom window. People say that the night is black, but they do not see like we see. We stood in the golden night while the dew soaked up our feet. You pulled me to the pavement, and we ran, and our wet feet left our trail behind us. It did not matter where you were leading me because I trusted you. "Be very quiet," you said, so we ran on tiptoe, fearing that our neighbors would wake up, old Mr. Snider with his army green bark, or Mrs. Lowenstein with her raspberry laugh. A mockingbird sang like it was morning. We watched his melody dance in the night. It was brighter than I had seen before, without the daylight to wash it away. We ran all the way to the golf course where our father hit white balls into holes when he did not want to come home to us. "Look," you said when our feet touched the shorn grass. "It is a good place to be." You let go of my hand and you threw your arms out behind you and you ran. The sprinklers sputtered awake and clicked red and orange circles of water. You leapt through them and said to join you. So I threw my arms back and ran like you did. We spun around and around in the water. Fireflies glowed above our heads, bright spots of darkness against the amber night. The grass was so soft I hardly felt it below my feet, and when I looked down I saw that we were flying, that our bare feet hovered in the air far above the grass. I did not know we knew how to do that.

We flew to a tree on the edge of the golf course. Now the tornado has torn it down, but that night it enveloped us. We landed on its branches, and once we were inside it the tree grew and became a world. Its branches thickened and twisted and stretched farther than we could see. It could have held one hundred children if we had asked it. We jumped from branch to branch. I remember the way you laughed yellow that night, like a sunflower in the summer or a bright sticky popsicle. You hooked your knees over a branch like you were a trapeze artist, and I did not worry that you would fall, because I knew that the tree would catch you. "Climb higher," you said. We climbed as high as we could, and the tree grew with us. We could not reach the top because there was no top. "Remember this night," you told me, like you were much older than I was.

I was not often afraid back then, back when we had colors. But some nights we huddled together in bed and listened to the sound of people yelling, and sometimes there were other worse sounds too, and the colors disappeared. That was fear, tall and empty, a body without a face who sometimes came in at night and did things to us that we tried to forget. Then I would look at you and see your breath hitting the air, and I would close my eyes and be unafraid again.

Now that the tornado has hit I do not see colors. To another person I would say that the world is gray, an old-fashioned movie, Kansas before Oz, but you know that gray is a color and like all colors can be beautiful and satisfying. To you, then, I will say that the world is colorless. I do not know how I still see anything. Perhaps you would know, but you are gone and cannot tell me.

At your funeral we did not bury you. Your body was not there. I wondered where it went. "He was not our son, but we loved him like he was," our mother said. Our father stood next to her, tall and silent. The rain fell because that is what rain does at funerals. I saw the drops floating in the air like small clear balloons, and when they landed they matched the grass and the tombstones and the trees and the dirt. They disappeared, and I wondered if they had ever truly existed. We threw dirt on top of your empty grave, as if your body were really there. "I will find you," I said, because I could not imagine the world that I saw.

The tornado still rings in my ear, from the place where my head hit the door. That sound alone brings color, but it is pale and faded and hardly a color at all.

Now I stand in front of a long road that stretches west. I think that if I drive far enough the colors will return, and if I reach the end of the road, past the mountains and the deserts, and they have not, I will step into the ocean, and I will swim out. I will swim until I can swim no more. My mother holds me before I leave. She is crying a wail that I cannot see but I can feel. I promise her that she will not lose me too. But I have to go, because maybe if I go I will find you again and we will climb trees until we reach the sky. "I have always loved you," she says to me. "Even when I could not protect you." I tell her I know and that it is not her fault, the tornado was too strong, and our family was too weak. "That is not all I mean," she says, and I say I know that too, and it is okay.

I drive without thinking, and I stop only for gas. I no longer eat food, and I do not pause to see the landscape, because without the color of sounds the world that I see is dim and blurred. I drive until I reach a great underground lake of acidic water. The water spews from the ground, and it kills everything around it. I step onto the dead earth. I hear the rush of the geysers that sound as barren as the land. The water feeds on the earth, gnawing and reshaping it every few years. A group of tourists ask me to take their picture, and I turn from them as if I cannot hear them. If they follow me I will say that I am deaf from a tornado accident. They should not want their picture taken here on this ashen terrain. Here there is no life.

I imagine that I am standing on the moon, and in every direction the surface is desolate and gray. Even the flag planted so boldly has now faded. I hear the shouts of my fellow astronauts, but their voices are hollow. They echo against miles and miles of emptiness. How can sound be seen when it has nothing to crash into? Maybe that is why the colors are gone. Maybe you were what they crashed against. I watch the steam that rises from the poisonous water. It hisses against the air. I turn away.

Do you remember when we first saw the ocean? It brimmed with life and color, so different from the dead lakes where I now stand. We wore swimsuits that hung off of our thin bodies, and we drove with our parents to the Gulf Coast, where every spring the birds flock from Mexico, pink and blue and gold spots in the rosy morning sky. We dipped our toes into the water. It was as warm as the air. It dissolved the sand from our legs. You pointed far into the distance, where the colors of the horizon became one, and you said, "I want to go out there."

"It is too deep," I said. "We will drown."

And you said, "We cannot drown." We swam as far as our arms would carry us. We swam until our mother called to us to come back, but before we returned we waited. We hung in the water like it was the sky and we were flying. Our heads bobbed, and we looked at the world, flat and endless and bright, and when the waves splashed their salt we watched it fly into the air. "This is how I want to die," you said. "I want the water to swallow me. I would not mind."

"Don't talk like that," I said. "It's creepy." You laughed at me and asked me what was the color of death. I said I did not know. I did not have a color for it yet, but hovering in the water that summer afternoon, far from the shore and alone with you in the world, I knew that death was not colorless. Now I drive west toward the ocean, and I wonder if I will learn at last the answer to your question.

I am driving now through the mountains, higher and higher. At the top I can see summer snow, and I wish we could play in it. I think you would have liked snow. I think you would have turned it into a castle that was tall and strong and sparkling. You would have made yourself king, and there we could have ruled. The mountains stretch out in front of me, and I know they must be beautiful, but I cannot see it. I want to speed through them. Once I have reached the other side, perhaps the world will begin again to turn with the sounds that I remember seeing. High above me I see the ridge of the continental divide. I hear your voice in my memories. "Come with me," I hear you say, and I must climb. I park my truck, the one that used to sputter coughs of russet. I pull on a sweatshirt and begin climbing. The wind blows. It twists into my lungs and pulls out my breath. I choke, but I do not stop climbing. The trees fade away, and my skin cracks in the cold, dry air. I clutch at rocks to keep from falling. When I climb everything hurts—my lungs and my knees and my head from the tornado. The wind rushes into my ear and echoes in my head so loudly that I feel blind. I stumble to the top and stand on the mountain's ridge. Below me the earth stretches out with pools and hills and trees that have been bleached away. I yell. My voice echoes, and I imagine what it would have looked like once, the colors bouncing from mountain to mountain. Why did we never fly here to watch, you and I? When I have yelled everything I know how to yell I stand and wait. And he comes. A solitary swallow. Struggling against the thin air, thousands and thousands of feet above the sea. For a moment I see a flash of blue that is as bright as I remember colors being. He flutters across the divide, and he is gone.

My truck winds through the foothills. I drive quickly because night is coming soon and I do not want to be trapped. I think about the swallow. I wonder where he came from and how he survived so far away from any other life. I think about him, and I think about you, how both of you came from nowhere and lived where you were not supposed to be and then were gone. I am almost to the other side when I pass a woman who shivers next to her car with her head in her hands. I want to keep driving, because I am so close and I am not on this journey to meet strangers, but she is alone like I am now, and so I back up.

"What's wrong?" I ask. She says that her car is out of gas, and night is coming soon, and she is so, so afraid. Her voice blends with the mountains, colorless like the world around her. I tell the woman it is okay, I am here, and I will help you.

"How can you possibly help me?" she asks. "Even if you drive me somewhere safe I will be stranded there. I will be trapped."

"Don't be scared," I say. I hold her hand and I lead her to my truck. One night when we hid in the closet you held my hand like that. I was afraid of the things that were about to happen to us, but you weren't. "Why aren't you frightened like me?" I asked you, and you smiled at me like you understood something that I did not, as if nothing could really quite touch you. I lead the woman to my truck, and I give her my sweatshirt because she looks cold. She shakes as the chill flees her body and she thanks me. The hood frames her face like a mane. Her teeth chatter when she speaks, although the night still feels warm to me. I ask her where she is coming from. She says she lives down the mountain a ways. She does not say why she is traveling. I look at her and wonder what color she would have been. I can see it faintly, a washed-out blue that shimmers above her head.

We drive down the mountain. I want to keep her talking, but I do not know what to ask. The questions I used to ask you sound so silly now. Where are the other parts of me? Do they live in another universe? Why are the moments between sleep and waking the truest moments of the day? Will we be able to fly too far one day and never come back? I ask her instead, "Would you like something to eat?" She nods, and I pass her a bag of potato chips. She crunches them and licks the salt from her fingers, but she does not ask for water.

Night falls. The air cools, and the gas light in my truck blinks to life. When the woman sees it she wrings her hands and I think she might cry. "It will be okay," I tell her. At the base of the mountain we see the dim light of a bar. "See," I say. "There is nothing to worry about." We pull up to the building. Inside it looks like every other bar has always looked—chipped paint and dirty counters and country music that sounds like an empty tin cup. I ask the bartender if there is a hotel in town or somewhere we can stay, and he names a place and asks if we want a drink. On the far side of the bar a group of men sit with whiskey in their hands. They turn to us, and one man stands up.

"It's you," he shouts. "Where the hell have you been?" The woman cowers. She ducks behind me, although my body is still small like a child's body. When the man steps near, his face disappears, and I know that he would be colorless, even if I had not hit my head in the tornado. His arms are bare and cold. He wears heavy boots. "You're coming back with me," he says to the woman. "You are my wife," and when he says that it is a sentence with a gavel.

"Come with me instead," I tell the woman. She cannot hear me. For her, fear is deaf. I touch her arm and she jumps away. I wish that you were here, because you always knew how to call me away from the things that were hurting me. But now it is just me, and I must do this alone.

"Listen to me," I say. I tell her that I do not know who this person is, but she does not have to go with him. I tell her that I will take her wherever she wants to go. The man glares at me and asks me who do I think I am, but he does not know that I cannot see his face. I take the woman's hand, like you used to take mine, and I pull her with me out of the bar. "Run," I tell her, because I know what happens when we run. She runs with me, over the mountains that are dark and still. I look down to see our feet, but we are not flying. We stay on the ground. Still we run, even if we cannot fly, under the lamplight of the sleeping town. We run as far and as fast as we can, until we are safe, until everything is right and there is no more fear. "Will you be okay? Can you go on alone now?" I ask the woman, and she nods, and she says through her panting breath that she is brave enough now, although I know that she was brave all along.

When we went camping, the animals crowded around you. We could talk to them. We could read their colors and they knew our thoughts. We crept out of our tent in the early morning, while our parents were still sleeping, and we tiptoed through pine needles so that no one would wake up. We sat at a stream. A turtle nuzzled your leg, and you stroked his head. A woodpecker sat on my arm with his chest bright red and yellow. A flock of sheep came to drink from the creek, bleating rose petal cries of pink and orange, and when they saw us, they were unafraid.

"What will happen when we are old and our skin sags and our eyes are foggy?" I asked.

"Hush," you said, because whoever you were, and wherever you came from, you were not worried about the things that worried me. We heard our parents waking up and wondering where we were, and our father's voice grew louder and yelled for us until it paled, but you told me that whatever happened when we got back, whatever anger or darkness we must face, we could survive, we were strong. So we buried our faces in the animals' fur, and we forgot everything else.

I drive to the coast. It is not the Gulf Coast with its bright birds and warm, sticky air. This coast fills my body with cold. I walk over the rocks crusted with the sea, and one pierces my foot. My blood mixes in the cold water and turns gray. Clams shoot saltwater into the air as they burrow underground. I shiver and wrap my arms around myself, as if they were enough to warm me. In the distance a boulder towers in the sky. I climb it, and when my knees scrape against its side and my skin is peeled away I feel nothing. Standing on top of the rock I can see for miles and miles. I see the orcas that leap high above the sea as if they are trying to escape its pull. I see the fishing boats that catch salmon to ship across the country. I see pelicans and great blue herons that swoop to the ocean to steal fish for their young. I feel the coast groan beneath me at the endless struggle of death that sustains life. I remember the woman, alone and free now, courageous, and I remember the swallow flying strong through the thin, cold air, and I remember you. I climb down from the rock.

Now I step into the ocean. The tornado ringing in my ear absorbs the sound of the waves. I watch a faded jellyfish squirm past, and I reach my finger out and touch it. The salt foams at my ankles. I do not know what I will find when I swim out. I still hope that somehow, at the end of something, some height or some depth or some distance, I will find you again. That you will hold my hand and we will watch the colors of the world dance around us like we once did. That all I must do is swim far enough, or climb high enough, or fall deep enough.

But maybe at the world's end I will find life without you. Maybe I will find that a colorless life is bearable, that I can be strong, even when my feet no longer fly and the world does not grow and spin and change just for me. And so I swim. I am unafraid. I swim to whatever waits for me. I swim until I am no longer cold, until I am no longer tired. I swim until the boulder is only a pebble in the distance. And when I think I can swim no more, I stretch out my fingers and pull myself one more arm's length, into the horizon.

PLEDGE

During my first September of teaching the school district deposited crawdaddies in my classroom as part of its third-grade science curriculum, as if I didn't have enough to juggle already. Most of them died right away. It became a sort of game for the children, checking each morning to see how many were floating lifeless in the water. By late September we had only two left, but they were strong ones. The students named them Julio and Josie.

I was a bilingual teacher in Texas, and I was in over my head, not truly bilingual, just good at interviews, teaching the lowest third-grade class in the lowest school in the district, students who should have been held back years ago, should have been diagnosed with things like ADD and dyslexia but weren't because all of that paperwork begins in third grade.

In Texas back-to-school signs and sharpened pencils don't mean changing leaves and cooling temperatures. It was a hot afternoon when Alexis invited me to his birthday party. He was my last student left for the day, and I sat at my desk finishing paperwork while I waited for his aunt. Alexis' little sister was sick, so I told his aunt I'd keep Alexis late when she needed to take her niece to the free clinic. Alexis didn't have a mother that I knew of, and I'd never seen his father. That afternoon he sharpened pencils and chattered to me. "Some day I am going to be a soccer player," he said, and I asked him how often he practiced. "I don't need to," he said. "My people, soccer is in our blood."

I smiled at him, and I said I hoped that worked out. I didn't mention his limp, his clubfoot. He offered me a Takis. "Quieres probarlo," he asked me, and I said no, I didn't want to try.

"No me gusta comida," I paused. "Come se dice 'spicy'?"

Alexis shrugged and licked bright red powder off of his fingers. They were getting used to my lack of Spanish. They helped me fill in the words I didn't know how to say, but already I felt guilty, guilty that I couldn't communicate with them more, that of all the bilingual classrooms in the school, they'd ended up in mine. I was working as hard as I could to learn the language, staying up late most nights after teaching, and I was sure it would come, but it was taking a long time.

The fourth-grade bilingual teacher stuck his head through the door. "Hola, Maestra," he said, and he grinned at me. Jose Pablo had taken me under his wing. He was a good teacher with students who tested well. The other bilingual teachers stood behind him chattering in Spanish too quickly for me to know where one word ended and the next began. Jose Pablo, the most fluent in English of the group, often translated for us. "We are going out for drinks. Want to come?" The other teachers nodded their agreement. I appreciated how they tried to include me, but I wasn't close to any of them, felt more comfortable with my students who accepted my broken Spanish in that easy way children have. Jose Pablo's wife Rosario was sweet and perhaps could have made a good friend if we had been able to communicate better. Jose Pablo had met her in Mexico, where he had been a priest. After they fell in love he left the church and they moved to Texas to fill the school's fourth and sixth-grade bilingual positions. Ismael was another first-year teacher, like me. The school had recruited him directly from Mexico and found him housing near campus. Now he was already winning awards at our Wednesday afternoon school meetings while I still struggled to conjugate verbs and tell my students to walk quietly to music class.

"Hola, Alexis, qué onda?" Ismael said. Alexis turned to him and limped over to give him a high five. Ismael was young and energetic, and he spoke Mexican slang, and my students loved him.

"I'm sorry," I said to the bilingual teachers. I told them I would love to go, but I had paperwork to finish, and I was tired.

"Maestra," said Alexis when they were gone. "You should go with them. They can be your friends." I smiled at him and once again felt that guilt. He was such a bright boy. He would have done well with a truly bilingual teacher.

I hadn't always wanted to be a teacher, not like so many of my colleagues had. I'd been raised by my grandparents, born to a mother who was too young to raise me herself. I'd only met her a few times; if I had any siblings, I'd never met them. It was just my grandparents and me. But my grandfather had died of kidney failure while I was in high school, and now my grandmother was in a nursing home in the early stages of Alzheimer's, and I would soon be alone. And so I became a teacher. My students would become my family, I thought, and I would become theirs. We would help each other. We would belong.

Alexis asked if he could clean the classroom. It was crowded and cluttered, Spanish signs paired with English, pencils shavings staining the white linoleum gray, books lying sideways on shelves. He righted a copy of *Jorge el Curioso* and displayed it on a shelf next to a stuffed Curious George I had found at a thrift store last summer, back when I'd felt more hopeful. I stood by the window and looked out at the parking lot, the brown grass, the blinding reflection of the sun off the teachers' cars. My head hurt, the languages in my brain fighting to merge. I hadn't known I would be so exhausted, teaching and learning Spanish all at once, meeting the needs of my students, trying to help them succeed. Soon it would be easier, I hoped. Soon the Spanish would sink in, and my students' test scores would improve, and I would be one of them. On the counter below the window the pair of crawdaddies swam back and forth in their plastic tub. I'd promised the students we would have a lottery for the animals when we finished our science unit.

"Teacher," said Alexis. "Do you want to come to my birthday? We will have pastel!"

I told him I didn't know. "I'm pretty busy, but I'd like to," I said. "When is it?" It would be a good way to get to know my students, if I could fit it in. He said it was next Friday.

The day of the party I drove my Accord to Alexis' neighborhood, and I tried not to notice the houses growing smaller, the dogs roaming the streets, the smell of mold from un-raked leaves. I wondered what my grandparents would have said if they had seen me in a place like this, so different from the suburban home they raised me in. I knew Alexis' house by the green balloon tied to the mailbox and a sign written in letters I recognized to be his. The house was small, faded yellow with bushes that needed trimming and dirt instead of grass. Alexis must have seen me drive up. Before I turned off my car he opened the front door and ran to me. I knew all of his outfits by now, his stained sweatshirts and patched jeans, but today he wore a clean camo sweat suit with crisp, new colors, and he stood tall and proud. He hugged me, and I gave him the soccer ball I'd brought. "Thank you, Teacher," he said. He pulled the red bow off the top of the ball and stuck it on his head. "Do I look handsome?" he asked, and I said he looked the most handsome, and then he laughed and ran off to kick the ball to one of his friends.

I knocked on the front door, but no one answered, although I heard voices inside. I assumed they hadn't heard my knock, and so I went in. My eyes adjusted slowly to the dim light. A window AC unit churned out a steady stream of stale air. I slipped off my cardigan and put it in my purse. "Hello?" I said. "Hola?" A voice farther in the house called for me to come in, and I found a few women crowded in a tiny kitchen, prepping bright red meat and chopping onions. I gagged at the smells, the blood and the onion peels and the sweaty bodies. I wanted to turn away.

"Hola, Maestra, bienvenidos!" said Alexis' aunt. She introduced me to the other women in the kitchen and told them I was the teacher. They smiled at me, and I said "mucho gusto" and pretended I knew everything they were saying. One of the women tripped in the crowded kitchen and her hands left filthy smears of blood and grease on the counter where she caught herself. The women laughed loudly. An older women stood at the stove frying beans in a skillet filled to the brim with bubbling lard. It smelled of dead pigs and foods I did not ever want to try. Alexis had his gift, and I almost turned to leave. But then Alexis' aunt put a Pacífico beer in my hand and thanked me again for coming, and the other women joined in, and I was in the middle of them, the Spanish encircling me in a spell I could not understand but could feel, and I knew then I could not get away.

The backyard patio was filled with boys and girls and men and women, and here the smells were of lime and garlic and pineapple juice sizzling over flames, and of fruit—papayas and mangos and melons covered in chili sauce, like the food my students brought for lunch, the food they sometimes offered me but that I had never before accepted. A young-looking man, Alexis' father perhaps, stood at the barbeque grilling meat and passing it to a teenager to cut into strips. The women brought out warmed tortillas, and children filled their plates with meat and beans and onions. Alexis and some other children kicked his new soccer ball around the yard. I recognized Roberto from my class. His family had moved to Texas from Mexico this year, and he spoke no English. Their shoes were off, and Alexis kicked with his left food and limped a little bit, but his face was full of laughter, and I was glad that I had come to see that. The man at the grill turned to me and spoke in English, "He is a good boy, no?"

"Yes," I said. "Are you his father?"

"Antonio. Mucho gusto."

"Mucho gusto," I said. I hoped my accent wasn't too strong. When he smiled at me his eyes were as bright as Alexis' in those times he talked to me about soccer.

He asked me if I wanted some food, and he handed me a plate of carne asada and tortillas. His shirt stretched tight against his chest, his dark hair buzzed like Alexis'. Alexis would be a handsome man when he grew up, I thought. I wanted to ask Antonio something, to keep talking to him, but none of the things I'd often wondered about Alexis sounded polite—why his foot hadn't been fixed when he was a baby, what happened to his mother, how long the family had been in Texas and if they had come legally or through some great and dangerous adventure—so I asked instead if Alexis was on a soccer team.

"No. We tried when he was little, but they would not let him play much with his clubfoot. He has fun with his primos, though," he said, nodding toward the boy. I sopped up the tangy juice from the meat with my tortilla and hoped it didn't run down my chin. Antonio offered me a napkin.

"Yes, he looks like he's having fun," I agreed.

"Do you think he will pass the tercer grado?" Antonio asked me, and I told him with enough work, he was sure to pass; he was a smart boy. I didn't tell him that I was concerned, that I knew Alexis was bright but his reading was far below grade-level, that the next few months would require after-school tutoring and would perhaps lead to a diagnosis of dyslexia, although the diagnosis would do little to help Alexis since the district's dyslexia programs were all in English and bilingual children were taught to read in Spanish first. There would be time enough to discuss these things after the boy's birthday.

"Alexis!" Antoino called to his son. "Ven aquí."

Alexis came running, sweat dripping down his face. "Si, papi?" he asked.

"Show la maestra your new present," Antonio said. Alexis asked if I wanted to see it. He took my hand and led me to a small house behind the patio, no larger than a garage. Like the house, this space was dim, and smelled of sweat and bodies. I saw a bed and a dresser. A portable fan spun, and wind blew through two doors, but the room was still too hot. I wanted to return to the patio, but Alexis motioned me farther in. A sheet hung from the ceiling, dividing the home in two. Alexis drew it aside.

"This way, Teacher," he said.

"What is this place?" I asked. I didn't want to assume.

"My house," he said. "And the house of my father and sister."

I tried to hide my confusion from Alexis and from myself. I did not want to believe that my student lived here, crowded in with so many people. I wondered if it was legal, what city ordinances they were breaking. Then again, I didn't even know of his legal status in this country. Texas law prohibited me from asking, as his teacher. "And that house?" I asked, pointing to the house I'd entered.

"That is the home of my tío and tía and my primos," he said. Alexis plopped himself on a mattress and pointed to a poster hanging on the wall. "Look what my papi gave me for my birthday," he said. It was a poster of a soccer player. I didn't know which one, but the name read Ronaldo. Alexis pointed to a black signature at the bottom of the poster. "See, Teacher?" he said. "He firma'd it."

"That's wonderful, Alexis," I said, and I hoped that he wouldn't find out for a very long time that it was pre-printed. Alexis scratched at his foot, and I hoped too that he wouldn't find out for a very long time that he would never be a soccer player.

I sat down on the mattress next to Alexis and imagined living here. I wondered how he slept in the heat and if he got tired of being so near his father and sister, if any of them ever wanted privacy. I wanted to ask him these things, but perhaps he did not even know, himself. An empty plastic cage sitting on the floor by Alexis' mattress caught my eye.

"And what's this?" I asked.

"That is for a crawdad. I want Julio."

"Oh Alexis sweetie," I said. "You know we're doing a drawing for the crawfish when we finish the unit. Don't get your hopes up."

Alexis said he knew. "But I think I will win."

When we rejoined the party most of the guests were finishing their food, wiping grease on their shirts or licking their fingers. The sun was setting, and the night was cool. A breeze blew through the patio, and a string of lights hanging from the trees twinkled. Toddlers chased each other and squealed when their mothers swept them up for the next game. Alexis' aunt lowered a piñata shaped like a soccer ball and handed Alexis a plastic baseball bat. The children sang a song I did not know. "Dale, dale, dale," they sang, and each time the children told him to "hit it," Alexis whacked at the air while his father raised and lowered the piñata. Alexis' uncle gave me another beer.

The adults were clapping along now, singing with the children: "Ya le diste una," they sang. "Ya le diste dos. Ya le distre tres. Y tu tiempo se acabó."

Alexis shrugged when his turn ended and took off his blindfold. He gave the bat to the next child in line, and the song began again. I looked at them, all of them. Two women stood next to each other; they looked like sisters, with long, colorful skirts and hair just beginning to turn gray. I wondered if I looked like any of my half-siblings, if they existed. The larger sister nudged the other and pointed when one of the children almost hit the piñata. Her eyes looked proud, the way I had seen mothers looking at their daughters, the way sometimes my grandmother had looked at me, before the dementia. The other sister laughed, and they both clapped their hands for the little girl.

Some of the men stood near Antonio and helped him guide the piñata away from the blindfolded children. They cheered when the children struck air and clapped Antonio on the back. Although they teased the children, I saw their pride too, the mothers and the fathers and the uncles and the aunts. These children were their world. And I was their teacher. In that moment, I belonged, and felt all the weight of belonging.

Antonio motioned me over and handed me the bat. "Want to try?" he asked. He took my beer, and the parents cheered for me. I didn't know if they were native Texans or recent documented or undocumented immigrants, but they had all sacrificed something for their children to be here learning from me. I was supposed to teach them English and reading and math, and maybe offer them a chance at college. Alexis took my hand, wouldn't let me go. He put the blindfold over my eyes and spun me around.

"Open it, Maestra," he begged. I swung once, and then again. On the third swing, I struck. The children yelled, and the song stopped. Within seconds the piñata was on the ground, a crowd of children clawing on top of it. They sucked on sweets that I recognized from teaching, things like chili-covered peanuts and lollipops shaped like corn. I stepped back and Alexis' father touched my shoulder. "Nice job," he smiled. Then Alexis ran to his father to show him his candy. "Wow, Mijo!" Antonio said. He picked the boy up and threw him into the air even though he was nine years old now. Alexis laughed, and his candy fell to the ground.

I had work to finish the next morning, so I woke early to drive through empty Saturday streets. The building was locked, but I had a key to the back door near the playground. I let myself in and walked through dark hallways plastered with motivational posters and student work. The crawdaddies were still alive in my classroom. Josie had shed her shell during the night, and it looked like a third crawdad was lying dead in the plastic tub. I changed the water so the room would not smell.

I tried to finish paperwork, but I couldn't focus. I wondered how many of my students lived in small rooms like Alexis, their mattresses pushed underneath parents' beds during the day, their clothes and belongings stuffed wherever there was space. I wondered how many of them had enough to eat, how many lived in fear of deportation. I pulled out my students' cumulative folders that followed them from grade to grade, and I checked their addresses for the first time that year—some in apartment complexes, many in a nearby trailer park, a few listed as homeless. I saw their diagnostic test scores, the ones I was challenged with fixing once I learned enough Spanish. I remembered the way I had been welcomed the night before, into a world I wasn't rightfully a part of, and I wanted so badly to repay them, to give them all what they had come to this country for. I would spend every minute studying, I pledged. I would help them all, and in that way, we would become family.

Behind me I heard the scurry of claws in the crawdaddies' tub. I spun my chair around and looked at the ugly creatures. I'd eaten them piled high on butcher paper with my grandparents. But Alexis wanted Julio as a pet, and this was a small dream I could make real. The crawdaddies swam in circles until they hit the edge of the cage. Julio wriggled his pink body and stretched his front claw out to pinch at the air.

I drove to Alexis' house. I hadn't told him I would be coming. I wanted the crawfish to be a surprise. Julio sat in the passenger seat in a yogurt container filled with yellow water, and I drove slowly so it wouldn't spill in my car. I didn't know whether or not to knock at the main house, but it looked empty, so I walked around back. "Alexis?" I called, and I knocked on the door.

Antonio answered. He wore jeans and a white undershirt and held a beer, and I could see sweat on his hairline. "Excuse me, Maestra," he said. He explained that he had just finished an early shift with his crew.

"On Saturday?" I asked, and he said every day.

"I work hard," he said. I said that was fine, I didn't mind the sweaty clothes, and I asked where Alexis was.

"I brought him a present." I held up the crawfish.

"Alexis will be so happy," Antonio said, but he was sorry, Alexi was with his aunt. They were at the clinic again. "They will be home soon, though. You want to wait?"

I told him I would, maybe just a few minutes, and Antonio motioned that I should sit down on the bed. He popped the lid off of a Corona for me and squeezed limes and Tabasco sauce inside the bottle. I swallowed the beer and tasted the tangy spice. Sweat ran down my back. I hoped Alexis would be home soon. "Does this place get cooler in the fall?" I asked. Antonio laughed and said you get used to it. He asked me what my story was, did I grow up here or what, and I told him yes, I'd been raised in Texas and lived here my whole life.

"You must be used to the heat then?" he said, and I said I guess, but not like this.

"Can I ask you a question?" I said. "What happened to Alexis' mother?"

He took another sip.

"I'm sorry if that's too personal," I said.

"No, todo bien," he said. "She died in Mexico. It's when I knew it was time to come here." He didn't offer any other details, and I didn't ask.

"Have you been to my country?" he asked. I shook my head and said no, but I wanted to, and he asked, "Then why do you not go?" He pulled a photo album from under the bed and flipped it open. "My country, it is beautiful. Look," he said. "You will love it." I finished my beer. The last few sips were warm and left specks of lime and Tabasco on my tongue. I said maybe I should be going. But Antonio put his hand on my arm and said, "Please stay," and he gave me another beer and flipped through photos of crowds of people, men and women and children in a land filled with mountains and a white burning sun.

"Look at this one," he said. The picture he pointed to was green and beautiful, a waterfall splashing into a creek. "This is my home," he told me. "Oaxaca. My hermano and me, we used to play here in this cascada." He told me how his mother would take them to play in the water in the summer months, when the sun heated their concrete home like an oven. I imagined two brothers playing in the water. I imagined them ducking their heads under the waterfall, laughing the way I sometimes saw siblings laughing. "If you visit Mexico, you must visit this place," Antonio said. I thought of my grandparents, wondered what they would say to see me sitting there, but they were gone now, or nearly.

He found another picture, of another waterfall, this time tall and majestic, spilling down a high mountain. "This is Hierve el Agua," he said. "It looks like a waterfall, but it is really minerals that have hardened."

"It's beautiful," I said, and he told me how you could hike there, through the springs, and swim high up in natural pools that overlooked the valleys and the hardened mineral waterfall. He told me how you could dangle your feet off the white cliffs and let them hang hundreds of meters in the air. Texas has no place like this one, is what he told me.

He flipped the pages in the photo album to another picture. I told him to wait while I got another beer from the refrigerator in the garage. It was cold, and the room was still hot, and I drank quickly. "This one is of the huelga, the strike," Antonio said. He explained that every year the teachers line the streets of town and strike for better working conditions. "Oaxaca is very political," he said. "My prima, she is a teacher there." He told me how his cousin asked the family to come strike with her, because no matter how hard she worked she couldn't make enough to live. He pointed to his cousin sitting under a tarp on the Oaxacan streets and told me how the family camped there all week long. The children played games and the parents visited with friends they hadn't seen all year and the tourists took their pictures. "They do not understand," he said.

"You miss it there," I said. He nodded. "Will you go back?"

"I gave it up to live here," he said. "For Alexis." I knew what that meant and how uncertain it made his future. I didn't press. He told me, "When you have a vacation you should visit. They will let you in." He was close to me then. His body was so near mine I could smell his scalp. I touched his hand.

"I'm sorry," I said, although I did not know what I was sorry for.

He acted like he didn't notice my hand, told me his parents were still there and said if I went, maybe I could stay with them, maybe I could live there all summer and practice my Spanish and see his home. It moved me, the way he welcomed me into his world, made me feel like I belonged.

"Maestra! Hola!" Alexis stood in the doorway. I pulled my arm back, scooted away from Antonio and his warm breath.

"I brought you something." I held the crawdad out to Alexis, and his eyes lit.

"Did I win?" he asked. I told him he had. We filled the plastic cage with tap water and lowered Julio in. He swam to the edge, tapped his claws against the side, turned around and swam back. Alexis laughed.

"You have made him very happy," said Antonio. "Gracias."

We were all three squatted around the cage on the floor, and it must have been the heat, or the beers, or the long hours he'd already worked, because Antonio reached out and put his hand on my leg. I didn't say anything, but I took his hand and swallowed a smile, and I thought, there is room for me here. Here was a place I could belong. Here was a need I was suited to fill at last. I put my hand on Alexis' back. "I'm glad you're happy," I said.

That weekend I saw our family, my family. I saw Antonio and Alexis, Alexis' little sister, me, one of them, cooking them breakfast, helping Alexis with his homework, telling Antonio to be careful at work. This was why I had become a teacher, to belong to someone. I hadn't expected it to happen like this, but life could surprise you.

I was at school early Monday morning. I thought maybe Antonio would drop Alexis off, and I wanted to be ready for him. Maybe he would invite me home after work. I would get tomorrow's prep finished just in case.

Alexis never showed, though. It wasn't like him to be absent. I gave the children longer than usual to finish their bell work, hoping he'd come, my eye on the door. Was this because of me? Should I have ignored his hand on my leg, moved away from him, shown him I wasn't trying to take his wife's place?

Josie wasn't doing well. The children crowded around her all day.

"Have any of you seen Alexis?" I asked, but they said they hadn't, didn't know why he was absent.

"Will Josie be okay?" asked one student. Another wondered what happened to Julio.

"Maybe she wants to be free in the creek with the other crawdaddies," said a girl.

I told them that was a good idea. Maybe we would release her during recess. But I knew that if we put her in the creek she would die there too, destroyed by bacteria she had never learned to fight off or eaten by predators. Either way, her days were numbered.

Alexis didn't return on Tuesday, and then again on Wednesday. I called his home and left messages. I even went to his house, knocked on his garage apartment door. No one answered, though, and then I worried they were hiding from me and I was pushing too hard. Maybe I should let them return on their own time, take things slow, or start over.

A week later, though, and Alexis still wasn't back. Another student was placed in my class, a little girl transferring in from another district, and my roster online changed, showed her name instead of Alexis'.

"What happened to him?" I asked the secretary. "Will he be coming back? Did his father request he move to a different class?"

"He's gone," she told me. "Deported."

Back in my classroom the morning announcements came on the television, and my students turned their eyes to the screen. Two of Ms. Miller's students from down the hall were chosen to give the announcements this morning. Texas may have desegregated its schools decades ago, but Ms. Miller's class looked nothing like mine, and my class looked nothing like the classes in the wealthier neighborhoods in the district. White and black and Hispanic, still as separate as they ever were. I didn't belong in this room. No amount of language study could change that. My life would never be theirs. I knew this now, suddenly, and should have known it before.

"Please stand for the Pledge of Allegiance," the student announcers said. I heard chairs scraping the linoleum floors from every classroom in the building as students rose to their feet.

"I pledge allegiance to the United States of America," the school chanted.

My students read aloud from a poster near the flag. I wondered if they knew what those English words meant. Pledge? Allegiance? It was probably my job to teach them, but what would I say? When you recite this you are promising that you will be loyal to this country forever? I thought of Alexis, the way he always strained to read the words on the poster. He should have been tested for dyslexia years ago. I thought of his crowded home and the way his father hoped he would pass third grade, how I would never see either of them again, just like that.

Maria Victoria was scratching her leg. She lived in the apartment complex near the school, the one the white teachers were afraid to visit. Roberto from Alexis' party lived there with her. He came to school with his hair slicked back straight every morning, his face serious, and when we recited the pledge he still held his elbow high and his palm parallel to the floor in what he told me was the Mexican salute. Jaime was staring at the flag without blinking. His folder didn't list an address. Homeless perhaps, or staying with a relative. Natalia was in foster care, an American citizen whose family, like Alexis now, had been deported.

"With liberty and justice for all," the children finished. Ms. Miller's students said to remain standing for the customary moment of silence, and my students were quiet. Behind us the crawdad thumped against the walls of her tub.

STATUES

We built them in every plaza, large packs of horses and our favorite presidents and the founders of our cities. They reminded us of our history, they kept us grateful and proud to be who we were. They were beautiful to look at, and powerful and strong, and we picnicked in their shadows.

How were we to know the danger? We expected it from so many places, rising oceans and incurable diseases, but not from this. We weren't prepared.

The day the statues came to life, we hid inside and watched through windows. In Texas herds of mustangs stampeded into buildings. Down in Mexico, monks swept through the streets, and their footsteps split the sidewalks and sent spiderweb cracks up the buildings. Over in Italy Old Testament heroes hunted and fought each other. Back in El Paso, Oñate rode through town on his giant horse and began conquering again, chopping off the feet of his captors, enslaving children, and we wondered why we had commemorated a war hero with a ten-meter statue.

We decided to fight. We had built these creatures, and we could destroy them. And so we organized. At first we formed small cells of soldiers, met in underground tunnels and caves, sent messages by carrier pigeons and courageous horsemen. We pulled old cannons from museums and stood side-by-side armed with shotguns and golf clubs and shovels. We held hands and yelled, "Come and get us if you dare!" It felt like something, to be united against these creatures we had built, to face our own history hand in hand and say to it, "Come and do your worst. We are ready."

We chose ourselves a leader; some joked and called him Jack the Giant Hunter, as if he could climb a magic beanstalk and slay the giant and return peace to us. He represented everything we loved about ourselves, our strength and our intelligence and our fortitude. With him leading the charge we almost felt proud that we had created these monsters. We were powerful enough to destroy the world, and so of course we must be powerful enough to save it.

The day before we went to war we slapped each other on the back. "It's almost over," we said. "Soon we'll have our world back." We talked about building a big statue for Jack after the war was won, five times the size of life, built of iron or bronze or even gold, and we all laughed at that idea. Our statue-building days were over.

We sat around our campfires that night, hidden far from the statues, and sang songs. We sang about the hard days behind us, the victory that was sure to come. We drank wine and told stories and ate our fill, our final preparation for the morning's fight. We went to bed with one another, made love without fear, because tomorrow the statues would be gone and the children we created would grow up in a safe world, a better one, where we had learned our lesson and lived wisely and in plenty.

The fight when it came was no fight at all. The statues smashed through our barricade, crushed our weapons. They stomped through our camps and destroyed our tents and food and possessions. We scurried around their feet and shot bullets upward, but the bullets ricocheted off their chests and wounded us instead. We fired cannons at a few of them, and the cannonballs were enough to crumble the statues, but after we had fired the last we had nothing left to use, no secret weapon or magic spell that would turn the tables and give us the victory. We prayed to our gods, but they were silent, or worse, they stomped against us with the other statues we had carved. So we ran for our lives.

In hiding, we watched the world crumble. The statues traveled the streets unchallenged, on stone legs we had carved and enormous steeds we had chiseled. They broke and tore and destroyed our world, and it felt like we were doing it to ourselves, because from deep in our hiding places we knew we were to blame.

Now the statues roam. We scurry around them. Most of us have taken to the countryside, and the statues chase us farther and farther away from our old life each day. We scavenge as much as we can for the children we bore, soothe their cries when they are hungry, carry them on our backs when they are tired. We tell them stories of the world back before the statues. Back when gardens grew and businesses thrived and the cities were ours. Back when we ruled the earth, and we marked our rule with monuments in every plaza.

This is how the world ends.

With giant bronze bulls crashing through Wall Street, stone lions roaming the streets of Chicago, soldiers riding on horseback across Russia, gargoyles flying through Europe. With the slow, steady stomp of giants, the mountains crumbling, the prairies splitting in two.

CARNIVAL RIDE

We didn't come for you that morning because the abandoned carnival blocked the intersection—merry-go-rounds and bumper cars and pirate ships strewn about like something in an apocalypse film. Your school called us. They told us about the bomb threat, that we needed to come pick you up right away, but the spinning teacups blocked our path, their pink and blue and yellow bright in the gray dawn. Your father called his friends, and they called their friends, and everyone came to help us lift. The sun rose behind the volcano and shone onto the street and made the sweat bead beneath our shirts.

You were born with two colors in your eyes, the child of two countries, irises a swirl of brown and green that confused our friends and family. You were the best of us, your father's jungles and beaches, my prairies and desert flowers. You laughed and the world was at peace, saw all that was possible. You were our life's work, our monument, stronger than rivers and the tallest of walls.

The day of the bomb threat, there was no bomb. There was only chaos, a frantic rush to get the children to safety, to send them home with anyone who would take them, an aunt or a nanny or a friend of a friend. And while we were lifting the spinning teacups beneath the mountain sun, and the school was packing children into crowded cars, someone came for you, and took you away.

You children can disappear so quickly. Your ties to the earth are so much looser than ours. I think you must be born with fairy wings, always poised, ready to fly away. You leave behind your soggy cereal and your unmade beds and your dolls and soccer shoes, but you take so much with you when you go, so much hope, promise.

I thought the world would dim without you. I thought it would grow quiet and pale. But instead it brightened. Helium balloons shone, and cathedrals' roofs sparkled gold, and bubbles floating in the air refracted the sunlight.

And then the city filled with clowns. They greeted us at airports and offered to carry our suitcases. They sat at the bus stops. They shopped in our grocery stores. They sang to us on street corners and thrust twisted balloons into our hands. They spilled into the intersection at red lights and circled our car with juggling pins. The whole town became a circus, white faces and rainbow wigs and painted smiles.

And so much noise, dogs barking on rooftops and trumpets playing in the square, everywhere people shouting and wanting to be heard. They banged sticks together on the bus. They screeched outside of cathedrals. They begged and sang and shouted and warned. They said that children were being blown up on the beaches, and more children were being starved in prisons, and raped in orphanages, and shot by gangs, and if you were a child the world was a terrible place for you to live, and I remembered how everything was quiet when you laughed, how your eyes shone with two colors and the code-switched language you spoke belonged to everyone but really to no one but you, and I know why you were taken. I know that the world was not ready, not for you, not yet.

I knew this would happen, I told your father. I knew that without her the world would splinter and crack, split right down the seams, fall apart in chaos and pain. And he took my hand and told me to come.

He took us back to the carnival. The street was empty now, no more vendors, no more traffic, no more pedestrians. Just the carnival rides, alone and deserted in the intersection, their gears rusted from the monsoons. Somewhere several blocks away a church bell chimed. Your father pulled me to the teacups, and he put a baseball bat in my hand. Swing, he told me.

Pretend the ball is the face of someone you hate, they used to say when I was a child trying to play baseball, but I never hated anyone then, not enough, and so I struck out every time.

But the carnival was everyone and everything that I hated, the nations that dropped bombs on each other's futures, the politicians who shoved their orphans into hidden institutions and left them to starve, the protesters at the borders who sent children back into the desert, the people who laughed at the swirl of colors in your eyes, the ones who took you from us. And so I swung. I swung like I was Babe Ruth or Willie Mays, hard enough to send a ball flying into the stands, hard enough to stop the teacups from ever spinning again. I swung, and the teacups cracked. They splintered, shattered, a million tiny pieces. The shards flew into the air above us, spinning and sparkling against the sun, and for a moment we saw reflected in them the beauty that is left in this world—the clouds, the sky, the hot, violent steam of the smoking volcano—and then they fell.

DÍA DE GRACIAS

The southern Mexican air smells of roasting chipotle peppers and empty bottles of Dos Equis. On the fire-spit, a tower of pork, onions, and pineapple spins. It's warm and comforting on a chill November night, but it's spicy warm, not apple cider and pumpkin bread warm. You slow as you walk past, let the fire heat your hands, watch a man carve charred bits of meat onto corn tortillas, flip slices of pineapple into the night sky and catch them, two slices on each taco. He motions at you to come inside and eat, but you shake your head and walk on.

This is home, but it isn't, and you don't think it ever will be.

You met him back in San Antonio when you were studying linguistics in college. He was sweet and polite and called himself Emilio. You and your friends went back to his family's restaurant again and again. "Field Work," you called it, studying the language patterns of recent immigrants. But your friends must have suspected that more than linguistics drew you to Mi Ranchera. Soon you were in love, and it was only then that Emilio told you he was undocumented, you and he could never be married.

For a few years that was fine. You hung your clothes in his closet and kept your toothbrush in his bathroom and said that paper meant nothing. But even though it didn't mean much, it meant something. You wanted to be the one the hospital called if Emilio had an accident. You wanted to know that Emilio would never be deported. If you ever had children you wanted them to feel safe, not hiding a secret their whole lives. So you talked to a lawyer. You explained that Emilio had come to Texas as a 14-year-old to work and send money back to his family, he had been a kid. The lawyer said your best shot was to be married in Mexico and then apply for a visa. Immigration would be lenient, considering the circumstances, he said.

Your parents were upset when you told them. Your mother wondered why you didn't marry first in the U.S. and then try to get a visa. "That's what the Alveras did," she said. "You remember them, don't you? They're such a sweet couple." You explained how that only worked when both people were in the U.S. legally, through a tourist visa for example. Since Emilio had entered illegally, he first had to go out before he could come back in.

"That's crazy," said your father. "Just don't tell them he came here illegally first and get him a green card."

"No, Dad," you said. "That's too risky. They would find out sometime when Emilio went to renew his visa and then we'd be deported. This is the only way to be sure."

He asked if you were certain you knew what you were doing. "Your career, your friends—you may never get all that back." You told him you knew. You loved Emilio and wanted to be married, and plus, he was sacrificing just as much for you.

So you gave up your country, and Emilio gave up his, and both of you moved to southern Mexico.

When you moved here you got a job teaching linguistics at the Universidad de las Americas in Cholula, a college town near Puebla built on top of ancient ruins, clubs, and casinos and pyramids sharing the same streets. Emilio had few options in this country, so he set up a corner restaurant in front of your house where he charged 40 pesos for a four-course meal. You were married. You mailed in your visa application.

Emilio is watching TV when you come home, his feet propped up on a tiny square coffee table. His beer is sitting on a school desk next to the couch. Since you would be here for only one year, maybe two, you collected odds and ends for furniture, unwilling to spend much for items you'd be leaving behind so soon. Old desks from the school for end tables and nightstands, an unfinished bookshelf from the antique market in Puebla, a mattress and box springs from a previous teacher who had gone back to the states. You decorated with some colored weavings and tin lizards you bought from the women selling crafts at the base of the pyramid on weekends. It all felt foreign, a costume you were forced to wear to a costume party you didn't want to attend, but it was only for a year.

Emilio asks you if you're hungry. He warms up the leftover food from his restaurant and hands you a plate of crepes covered in salsa poblana and crema. You sit next to him on the couch, kiss his cheek, ask him about his day.

"It was fine," he says.

"Did anyone come to eat?"

"A few people."

"Don't worry," you say, stirring the salsa and cream together until they become the palest green. "Soon they'll tell everyone how good your food is and you'll have the busiest cocina económica in Cholula." He smiles at you and says he hopes so. You think how handsome he is, how much you love his wavy black hair and the white burn marks on his hands from cooking.

You lean your head on him and take your shoes off. "Emilio, I want to celebrate Thanksgiving."

"Here in Mexico?" he asks. "But we have to work."

"I know. After work. Late. I can make the food earlier that week, and we can heat it up on Thanksgiving."

He asks why don't you celebrate on Saturday. "We can spend the whole day cooking, and it will feel more like the real thing."

You tell him it has to be Thursday. It won't be Thanksgiving if it's not on Thursday. Emilio laughs at you and says okay, he'd love to celebrate Thanksgiving with you any day you want. Then he says he has to start roasting cashews for pipián early tomorrow and he kisses you goodnight.

You lie next to him in bed and listen to the sounds of the night—a child cries through an open window, dogs bark on rooftops, bachata music plays down the street. You begin to worry. Your kitchen doesn't have a counter, so you usually cook on the table. That works for small meals, but Thanksgiving won't be small. You're still not even sure you know how to use your oven. First, though, you need to find a turkey and sweet potatoes and pumpkin filling and everything else that the supermarkets won't carry until closer to Christmas. You remember last Thanksgiving when Emilio came to West Texas to spend it with your family. They'd met him before, but only briefly, and you wanted them to know the man you were giving up your country for. He'd thrown the football with your brother Nelson and helped your father carve the turkey and won your mother over by the way he could roll out a piecrust. He fit perfectly, just like he'd been made for your family. But that was the last time you had all been together. Nelson hadn't been able to come down for the wedding in the summer, and now Emilio couldn't go back to Texas until his visa came through. This will be a good Thanksgiving, though, you tell yourself. You'll have to talk to your coworker Claudia, who grew up traveling between San Diego and Mexico and can locate products from the States better than anyone you know. Maybe Claudia and her husband will come over, and you'll have turkey and potatoes and pie if you can find them, and it won't be like home but maybe it will be close.

The last week of October Emilio is waiting at the kitchen table when you come home from work. "It came!" he says.

"What came?"

"The immigration summons. I'm going to Ciudad Juárez to be interviewed for my visa."

You grab the letter from his hands and read it. Emilio will interview one week from now. You take two beers from the fridge, clink their necks together, toast your good fortune. You can't believe how well things are turning out. The lawyer had told you to expect to wait for months and months, maybe even a year, but you'd moved down here only last summer. At this rate you'll be back in San Antonio by spring. Maybe Emilio would open his own restaurant there where he could really earn some money, and you'd be able to finish your doctorate in linguistics and get that tenure-track job you were planning on landing.

"This is perfect," you say. "November 8 is just two weeks before Thanksgiving. We'll really have something to be thankful for."

You spend the next week preparing for Thanksgiving and for Emilio's interview, and somehow the two meld into one, and you become certain that if you can learn how to make the perfect dinner rolls in this country then Emilio's interview will be perfect too and the two of you will be packing up for Texas before summer begins. Some nights you practice together. You bake while Emilio rehearses his speech, how he was a minor when he first entered the States and how he has worked hard and been a contributing member of society since then.

"Quiz me for my interview," Emilio says one night while you are kneading bread dough on the kitchen table, and you say you will as soon as you light the oven. You ask him what the exact altitude of Cholula is and you do an internet search for "baking at 7000 feet." You add more flour to your dough.

"Should I tell them that I wanted to work in the States when I was 14, or do I make it seem like my uncle took me against my will?" he asks.

"Be honest. You were a kid. You didn't know what you were agreeing to. They'll understand that."

The oven won't light. The gas line isn't clogged; you smell gas in your apartment. "Why doesn't this work?" you say. "There's gas in there, and now I'm putting a match in. Why doesn't it light?" Emilio tells you to be careful. "How can they rent us a house without a functioning oven, anyway?" Emilio says that people use stoves, he never remembers their oven working when he was a kid. "My mamá, she could make some amazing meals with her two burners, though," he says.

You turn the gas on again and close the oven door. It doesn't close all the way (you can smell the gas leaking out), but it closes enough. When you think it must have filled by now you crack the door open and throw a match in. A flash of fire and ears ringing. You jump back and check your eyebrows. "I hate this pinche country," you say, and Emilio laughs because you swear in Spanish now.

You'd said before you came that you wouldn't mind moving to Mexico. You'd been living in San Antonio for six years, and how different could it be? There was more Spanish than English there, you could eat mole in restaurants at 2 a.m., the supermarkets carried bolillos and jicama and helados. But everything feels off here, like walking through the world with your head sideways. The sidewalks are narrower, the traffic lanes more fluid, the voices louder, the buildings more colorful, the trees painted white, the candy covered in chile, the refrigerators shorter, the chips spicier, and there are dogs on the roofs and clowns sitting at bus stops.

You ask Emilio what he'll do first when he gets home. He doesn't say it much, but he misses the U.S., maybe even more than you do since he's not allowed back in. "I'm going to eat a huge plate of ribs covered in barbeque sauce. And then I'm going to wash my hands in the sink and drink straight from the faucet." You laugh and say it'll be nice to be able to open your mouth in the shower again.

"And our water will never run out halfway through a shower because we forgot to turn on the pump," he adds.

You sit next to him on the couch and watch the soccer game. Guadalajara is playing Chiapas. You can always follow the games without watching because the whole city cheers when Guadalajara scores. You eat some gringas that Emilio brought home after work, flour tortillas filled with cheese and pork and onions and pineapple and lime. Every flavor—spicy, salty, sweet, sour. You drink Coke made with real sugar. You never really liked Coke before moving here.

A cockroach waddles across the floor in front of the TV. You ask Emilio if he forgot to cover the drain in the bathroom again. "No, of course not," he says, but you don't believe him.

"I'll be glad when we don't have drains in every room in our house," you say as you stomp on the cockroach.

Another round of cheers fills the street. Someone somewhere bangs on a pot. You check the TV, Guadalajara is up by two. You say there's no point in trying to sleep until this game is over. You settle down into the couch, sprinkle chili on an extra lime and suck on it while Guadalajara wins.

Two weeks before Thanksgiving Emilio goes to Ciudad Juárez for his interview. You drop him off at the bus station in Puebla and say that you wish you could go with him but you have to teach. He is nervous. He holds his suit in his arms and you warn him not to hold it so tight or it will wrinkle. You tell him he'll do fine. He has nothing to worry about. "You're a good man, Emilio. You worked hard all your life for your family, even when you were a boy. You deserve that visa. They have to see that." He nods and says he hopes so, and then he gets on the bus.

You focus on Thanksgiving while Emilio is away. You call your mother and ask for your favorite recipes. "We're celebrating after work," you explain. "It won't be the same, but it will be better than nothing, and it's only for this year, we hope." She reminds you to put some lard in your pie crust to make it flaky, and you tell her that's the one ingredient you're not worried about finding. You ask Claudia for help during your lunch breaks at work, and she tells you to look for ingredients at Soriana. "When I'm missing the States, that's where I shop," she says. She teaches you the names for spices—nuez de moscada, and jengibre and canela and clavo, everything you'll need for your pumpkin pie and sweet potato casserole—and she warns you not too expect this Thanksgiving to be exactly the same.

"Oh, I know that," you say. "Of course."

You can't find a turkey in any grocery store. Whenever you ask they say they will get them in early December. Claudia suggests buying a chicken instead, since whole chickens are sold on nearly every street corner downtown. "Plus, do we even know if a turkey will fit in your oven?" she asks. You say maybe it won't, but maybe if you find a small one it will, and it has to be a turkey, who's ever heard of eating chicken for Thanksgiving?

Claudia tells you not to worry about it too much. "Once December hits people will start giving turkeys away as gifts, and you have to cook them right away because the freezers here are so small, so you'll have so much turkey it'll make you sick." You laugh and say you'd better start looking up recipes for leftover turkey, but it doesn't matter how much turkey you'll be eating next month because all that matters is Thanksgiving.

You thought you'd be able to find sweet potatoes without any problem, but the few you see at Soriana are shriveled and rotting. You try another store, and it's the same thing. You start thinking of Thanksgiving without sweet potatoes. All you need is turkey and potatoes and pumpkin pie to make Thanksgiving, Claudia says. But you know sweet potatoes are essential. You'll need two casseroles, one with marshmallows and one with nuts, plus the sweet potato pie. That'll take more than the four shriveled potatoes you were able to find. You ask the clerk if he has any more camotes. When he takes you to the camote bin in the produce section, you show him the rotten potato and tell him you need a lot. He goes into the back and comes out with a fresh box of camotes, skin tight over the bright orange flesh peeking through. You grab the box from his hands and thank him. "¡Muy amable! ¡Muchísimas gracias!" you say. He looks surprised, but you don't explain to him that this is the first time something has worked out perfectly since Emilio left for his interview. You dig through the box and pick out 15 of the best and can't help but hope that this victory means that Emilio's interview is going well.

Emilio returns Saturday night. He says he thinks it went well, but it's hard to tell. "They didn't ask me anything I hadn't prepared for," he says. "I think they were sympathetic when I told them about sending money to my family when I was a kid." You tell him that's the best news you've ever heard. You serve him a piece of sweet potato pie that you made for practice. The pie burnt around the edges in the oven, but underneath the crust is still flaky, and the sweet potatoes taste like changing leaves and hay rides. Emilio says it's the best he's ever had, and he kisses you with his mouth still full. You smile and say that everything will work out just fine.

On Sundays you and Emilio drive to Puebla to spend the afternoon downtown. It reminds you of a state fair back home. The air smells of fried food—empanadas and churros and fried platanos drenched in evaporated milk and chocolate sauce. Children chase pigeons, bands play music, and towers of balloons waltz above everyone's heads. You split a cup of esquites, roasted corn topped with mayonnaise and chili and lime. Emilio tells you that when he was a boy he refused to put chile on his corn and ate them with only mayonnaise. You say that's disgusting and that you wonder how he ever became a chef. You sit on the wall in the square and watch the clowns. A clown chooses five children from the audience and makes them lie on the ground so that he can jump over them. One little boy is scared and stands up crying. His mother picks him up and kisses him while the crowd laughs. You walk past the cathedral and cross yourself, like you've learned to do here whenever you pass a church. Emilio asks if you want to go in and you say yes. The cathedral was built in the 1600s, covered in gold, a sign of Spanish conquest, but now it is peaceful. You think it's more magnificent than the cathedral in Mexico City, even though it's not as well known. Once you're inside the world of

clowns and street vendors drifts to another universe. Far off someone
is yelling "empanadas de piña," but you're not sure that you hear it.
The children who were skipping rope outside the door a moment ago
now stand still beside their mothers. You look at the ceiling, domed
and painted and golden. Watch the women kneeling in the pews. Hold
your breath. Can breathing be irreverent? This is a beautiful country.
Why do you forget that?

The week before Thanksgiving you get the call. "We are unable to
approve Mr. Botello's visa at this time." Why not? Did he say something
wrong? Didn't they understand that he wasn't an adult when he entered?
Did they know that this isn't home? The answers were unsatisfactory.
Vague. There were complications. We merely process the information,
ma'am. How long then? When could he reapply? In five to ten years.

You go down the street to Emilio's cocina. He is silent when you
tell him. He looks at you, he holds out his hand, you put your hand
in his. He swallows and stares at the chiles poblanos he is filling with
steak and onions. When he finally speaks, all he says is, "I'm sorry."
You try to tell him it's okay, that you can be happy here and learn
how to make this your home, that being with him is all that matters.
But it comes out as "I'm going to check Soriana for turkeys again."
He follows you.
In the supermarket the Spanish is loud and distant. It melds into
a fog of sound, and you can't hear where one word ends and another
begins. The packaging is wrong, the spices have yellow lids instead of
black, the flour and sugar packages are too small—differences that
shouldn't matter but do. The fruits are too bright, too ripe and tropical.
The liquor section takes up three aisles and is in the front instead of the
back. Pyramids of Baileys and rompope are stacked near the checkout
for the holidays, and anyone can take free samples without showing an
ID. The world spins, but you think that it's probably just this world,
and that somewhere thousands of miles north it's standing still.

You leave. You forget to check for the turkey. You sit in the park. The tree trunks are painted a bright harsh white. The houses are pink and blue and orange. Will your children grow up thinking that houses are pink? Will they know that the whole world isn't so fluorescent as this? Five to ten years isn't so many. But what if you're settled by then and don't want to move back? This could really be home. Why do you hate that thought so much?

A gas truck drives by, playing the song that every child in the country knows by heart. Your children will know it too. When your gas tank is empty and you go for a day with cold showers and cold food they will know to run down the street to call the truck when they hear that song. A vendor offers you potato chips with Valentina salsa and lime. Your children will wrinkle their noses at crunchy potato chips that aren't turned soggy with the mixture. Maybe in a few months you'll wrinkle your nose at crunchy potato chips too. What will it be like, making a home in this country? Will you care about what's going on back in the States? Will it matter who's president or whether or not taxes increase? You're going to miss Cool Ranch Doritos and Cheez-Its and graham crackers.

Emilio sits next to you. His presence stops the whirl of wondering. "Let's find a turkey for Thanksgiving," he says. "It will be fine. It will all be fine." You wish you could hate him, this man who took you from your home. But you took him from his home too and he can never go back even though you can, and instead of hating him you feel indebted, and somehow that feels far worse.

After this, Emilio drives to every supermarket in Puebla, but none of them carry turkeys until December. He talks to the butchers at the carnicerías in Cholula. He comes home each night smelling like dead cows. You tell him the turkey doesn't matter and you even buy a chicken from the market downtown and store it in your freezer, but he says, "No, I'm going to get you that turkey if I have to drive to a turkey farm and kill one myself." When he says that you think of how the turkey farms are all in northern Mexico, close to the border. One night he tells you that you should just buy a plane ticket home for Thanksgiving. "Without you?" you say. You tell him he is being ridiculous and remind him that you can't afford a ticket at this short notice anyway. He shrugs and says maybe you can go home for Christmas. You are mad at him then. You ask him what type of person he thinks you are. Does he really think you would leave your husband on your first Christmas together after he got himself locked out of his country for you? "Don't say it like that," he says, and you feel bad because for a second you wonder if you might really be that person.

On Monday afternoon Emilio calls you at work. "I talked to my tío in D.F. and he says he found a man who will sell us a turkey." You start to say that Mexico City is too far of a drive, but Emilio interrupts you. "It's a real turkey," he says. "We can have a real Thanksgiving." You remember your father carving the turkey each year. One year you asked to do it, so he let you stand at the head of the table and showed you how to slice along the grain of the meat. Your family ate shredded turkey that year, but they said it still tasted good. You tell Emilio that he is wonderful, the best husband anyone could ask for, Thanksgiving will be perfect.

When he brings the turkey home you ask if it will fit in the oven. He holds it up. "I don't know. It's pretty big, like eight kilos," he says, and he smiles because he found it for you. You take it from him and open the oven door. It does not fit. Emilio holds the turkey for you while you move the oven racks around and try pushing the turkey harder. "Please fit," you say. Emilio puts it on the kitchen table and you try cutting part of it off with the largest knife you own, but it's too frozen. You slam the knife against the bird. "Can't just one thing be easy?" you yell.

"I'm sorry," Emilio says. He sets the turkey on the kitchen table.

"Oh, mi amor," you say when you see his face. You tell him it's not his fault, do not worry. This will work out because something has to work out for once, doesn't it? You tell him that he is perfect, you love him so much for finding the bird, and now you'll figure out how to cook it. You put it in your refrigerator because it won't fit in the freezer, and you start asking your coworkers if anyone has a modern oven that you can borrow. Claudia says her sister lives in a new fraccionamiento in Puebla that has American-style kitchens and she thinks you can use it.

You drive there the day before Thanksgiving during your mid-day comida break. You got up early that morning and prepared the turkey. You rubbed it with butter and romero, although you couldn't find thyme, and you filled it with stuffing made from Pan Bimbo you'd dried on your kitchen table overnight. Emilio asked you to sprinkle paprika on the stuffing because Thanksgiving food could be so bland. You'd told him it was supposed to taste bland, you were celebrating Thanksgiving, not Cinco de Mayo. "Come in," Claudia's sister says when you arrive. "Make yourself at home." You wonder if she has ever used her kitchen before. The oven is built into the wall and still has plastic wrap on its handle. The cabinets are large and empty. The stove is full, though. It has a griddle and a skillet and a saucepan on it, and you think those must be her only dishes. "Sorry, I don't do much baking," Claudia's sister says. You tell her that it's fine, that you are just happy to be able to use her beautiful kitchen. You type 475 into the Fahrenheit/Celsius converter on your phone, and you preheat the oven to 250 degrees and hope that this oven is accurate since Claudia's sister doesn't have an oven thermometer. Once the turkey cooks for 20 minutes you lower the temperature to 150 and say that you'll be back after work to pick it up.

You wonder about the turkey all evening. It has to be beautiful. It has to be perfect. When you return that night its skin has turned golden and crispy. It looks done to you, so you take it out and cover it with foil. You invite Claudia's sister to Thanksgiving but she says she doesn't like to stay out late on weeknights. When you get home you put your turkey back in the refrigerator and tell Emilio you cannot wait for tomorrow night.

On Thanksgiving you and Emilio argue about how to serve the turkey. He thinks you should carve it early and heat it in a pan before the guests arrive, but you tell him that the carving of the turkey is ceremony, and plus, he did such a good job of it last Thanksgiving at your parents' house. You tell him he should carve it cold at the table and then you can put it in the microwave for a few minutes while you serve the rest of the food. He agrees with your plan. You take off work to finish preparing. You hadn't planned on doing that, but now it seems important. You cover your table with flour and roll out piecrusts and peel apples and mash sweet potatoes and chop nuts. The pies burn around the edges and their insides are runny, but the rolls rise perfectly. You say, "Hey look, guess they weren't a metaphor for your visa." Emilio laughs. You can tell he's impressed and glad you're handling it so well. You talk to your family while you are baking. Your mother is trying a new pie this year. Your brother brought his girlfriend to meet the family. Your father says it's not the same without you. In the background you hear the Macy's parade, and you know that no one is watching it. You flip your TV on, but all that is airing on a Thursday afternoon is a telenovela. You leave it on for background noise. Teresa tells Mariano that his medical degree is taking too long and she will have to leave him.

Claudia and her husband come over after work, and they bring appetizers—sliced vegetables with chipotle dip, potato chips with salsa and lime. You pass around bottles of Negra Modelo and give the toast: "To Mexico!" "And Thanksgiving!" Claudia says.

When you sit down to eat it is already ten p.m. Everyone says the food looks delicious. They don't mention the burnt edges or the runny centers. Emilio carves the cold turkey. It shreds to pieces but you tell everyone that has happened to you before and it will still taste just right. You gather up the meat and stuffing and put them in the microwave. Claudia brought the mashed potatoes. When she uncovers them they are orange like sweet potatoes. "I put chipotles in them," she says. "Try them. You're going to love it!" The chipotles turn the potatoes smoky and warm. You wish you didn't like them, but you do and that's the problem. "These aren't bland at all!" Emilio says. "We're making some great new traditions." He goes to the kitchen and gets paprika to put on his stuffing. "May as well try this too," he says, and Claudia and her husband say that looks delicious.

"Think we could find some football on TV?" Claudia's husband asks. He flips through the channels. Only soccer. Someone makes a joke about real fútbol. Javier Hernández scores for Guadalajara, and everyone shouts, "¡Chicharito!" You serve sweet potato casserole. You made two of them, one with nuts and one with marshmallows. You searched through the bags of marshmallows at the store to find the one that had the fewest number of pink marshmallows, but you still ended up with some pink on top of your casserole. Emilio says that only makes it prettier, but you think that orange and pink don't match. You ran out of pecans, so the top of that dish is covered with walnuts and coconut. It turned black in the oven. You break through the nuts and spoon out the camotes. They taste of burnt sugar. You eat them anyway.

You eat until your stomach bulges. When everyone leans back and says they can't eat another bite you get up and bring the pies to the table. You serve slivers of each type and top them with the most ice cream-like product you were able to find. Claudia can't believe how much work you put into this. "She's been preparing for weeks now," says Emilio.

"It's Thanksgiving," you say.

When it's time for the guests to leave you pack them plates of leftovers. They thank you and say it was a perfect Thanksgiving, everything was delicious, let's do this again next year. "Except maybe on Saturday," Claudia says, looking at her watch.

You come inside and open another beer. Emilio is washing dishes. You tell him they can wait. They're not going anywhere.

He sits down beside you. "Tonight was good," he says, and that's all. You say yes and stand up. You go into your bedroom. He does not follow you. The drain is uncovered again. You cover it and check for cockroaches. You get into bed wearing all your clothes. From next door a mariachi band plays "Las Mañanitas" for a neighbor's birthday. "Despierta, mi bien, despierta," they sing. Wake up, my dear, wake up. You close your eyes and put your pillow over your head. After all these months you still haven't learned how to sleep through the noise. Bells ring from one of the town's churches. Claudia says every Christmas they tune the bells in the city to play a single song, a different note for each church. You will hear it this Christmas. Your children will hear it every Christmas. You will tell them about nativity programs and dressing up like sheep and angels, and maybe they will participate in one when they visit their grandparents in Texas, but they will always love the bell concert from their home the best, that will be their Christmas. You burrow down deeper, your head all the way under your sheets. They smell wrong, like detergent that's not yours and hard water. You get up and stand at the window. The November evening is cold and alive. The singing, the shouting, the smells of taco stands shutting down for the night.

DONATION

Body turned to bread, blood to wine. Broken, poured, consumed. Wafer placed on tongue, cup tilted to mouth. Ash smeared. Fingers raised to forehead, chest, shoulders, lips. Dust to dust. Life to death to life again.

She sees it written on the back of a pickup: Wife needs kidney. Mother of three. Blood type O. The traffic is still, the sunshine thick. She feels her kidneys heavy inside her, feels them purifying, filtering. She's always been interested in something like that, the giving of one life for another—a type of motherhood, or salvation. There's a number to call on the back of the truck, and she writes it down. She learns it's an easy thing to give away a kidney. The body hardly misses it at all. The mother she saves sends her pictures of the children through the years, birthdays and Christmases and graduations. "Thank you," the mother scribbles on the back.

When donated, if only donated in part, the liver will grow back, regain full function. There is a boy who needs hers, a little boy with curly hair and big eyes, who loves everyone without trying, who saves up his quarters to give to the homeless, feeds feral cats his leftover lunch on the way home from school. She sees his picture on the evening news, and she puts her hand under her right breast, where beneath her rib cage her liver breaks down insulin, stores the vitamins that give her energy, metabolizes toxins. She thinks of the poison piling up inside the little boy's body. She schedules the surgery.

She hates the word "hero" more than any other word. People remind her of the two lives she's saved. They tell her story with cocktails in hand, her sacrifice a party trick. They don't know what she has always known, that her body aches to be poured out, given away. That she can feel each of her organs inside her individually, full of life that could save others, and she longs to be rid of them. Her sacrifice is necessary, not heroic. If she could, she'd chop off her arms and legs, dig her eyes from their sockets, knock her teeth loose and wear dentures instead. She cuts off her hair for cancer patients. It grows back, so she makes the donation recurring. She visits blood donation booths weekly, offers her bone marrow and plasma. She takes iron pills, eats big red steaks and piles of spinach. The doctors say her blood is the richest they've seen, that it will save many lives.

There are ways to make oneself important, ways to change the world with passion and hard work. Some people serve in soup kitchens, cook food and wash dishes and hug strangers, and some raise children, teach them right from wrong, give them the education they need for success. Some move abroad. They build health clinics or dig wells or plant gardens. But she wants something that will cost her more than that. Something she can't have back.

A man writes asking for a lung. His letter is a prayer that lists the reasons he deserves to live, the recipient both his judge and savior. She loves to run. Her lungs have carried her to marathon finish lines, have pushed her over mountain trails when her feet have long wanted to quit. Her donated liver grew back, and her single kidney does the work of two, and the cells in her blood multiply and divide and replace, but with only one lung, she will gasp for breath the rest of her life, run slow little circles around the schoolyard track, content herself with participant medals. For the first time, she wants to tell the man no, her lung is hers to keep. But is a sacrifice that costs nothing truly a sacrifice? For the first time, she feels heroic.

The donations are easy after that, and fast, one after the other. She gives away her intestines and pancreas. She gives her skin, her bones, her stem cells, one of her corneas. Everything that can grow back. Everything she can do without. Her body spreads to others, goes into the world. More of it exists outside herself than within, and she likes to think of the life that was once her own, becoming new life, falling in love, raising children, burying grandparents, traveling to Paris and Cairo and Rome.

Her heart is the last to go. She has given everything else away but wants to give more. Besides, she is tired of it, the way it swells and falls, feels too much or not enough. It can do better work in a body that is whole. "Do you want to listen one last time?" the doctor asks before he takes it, and she holds the stethoscope to her chest, feels the cold against her many scars, listens to the heartbeats that kept her alive.

When she was a child she prayed to become a martyr, one for whom the world was not worthy. Her life was never taken from her, though, and so she will give it freely. There is no greater love than this.

The doctor places the mask over her mouth. He tells her to think of something happy, to count backward from ten. She closes her eyes and begins:

Ten. Nine. Eight.

She thinks of confession and absolution, baptism and rebirth. Remember that you are dust, and to dust you will return.

Seven. Six.

She feels the blood and nails in her wrists, the thorns in her forehead, the water in her side, the surge of love for this world and all who live in it.

Five. Four. Three.

Children sneak to the table and swallow the last drops of wine, stuff wafers into their mouths. Mice eat the crumbs. They carry the host away, the body and blood of our Lord spread throughout alleyways and sewers, across forests and fields.

ASTROMORPHOSIS

We were seven sisters. Hair the color of moonlight shining on snow-capped mountains, legs as straight and strong as the ponderosas in the hills. "The number of perfection," our father said, although we knew our mother disagreed. It wasn't that she didn't love us, but she worried. We were too young to worry back then, too happy just to be seven sisters living together in this world.

We became the seven colors of the rainbow. Back when we were small our mother sent us outside and we ran through the woods. We gathered wild strawberries and the red juice ran down our chins. We chased the sunsets, the hems of our skirts singed orange with its embers. We crushed marigolds between our fingertips and used the petals to perfume our necks with yellow. We planted seeds and watched the shoots spring from the dirt, green and full of new life. The earth was ours back then, ours to explore and enjoy and love. We climbed to the peaks of mountains and laughed beneath the welkin blue. We counted stars in the indigo pre-dawn night, and we rolled down hills blooming with lupine of every shade of violet. When we came home to our mother with scraped knees and torn dresses, she poured alcohol in our cuts and kissed our bruises and told us we must always stick together. "The world can be a cruel place," she said. "Some day you may have no one but each other." We crossed our hearts and promised her. It was an easy promise to make.

We became the seven notes of a musical scale, do re mi fa sol la ti. We could all sing each one, and we traded them between ourselves to make chords and arpeggios. We learned to harmonize, to tune our voices to sing major sevenths and diminished fourths. We couldn't keep silent, no matter how hard we tried. We sang and hummed and whistled. Sometimes our father complained about the noise, but we knew he really loved it. We could play instruments, but we didn't need to. Our voices were enough. We opened our mouths, and everyone turned to listen. One night we rode to the top of a Ferris wheel, and when the gears stuck and the wheel stopped turning, we sat in our basket high among the clouds and watched the colors of the carnival shining like spotlights into the sky, crimson and gold and lavender. One sister began to sing, and then another, and then another, until we were all singing, all seven of us as one. Everyone joined in, first on the Ferris wheel and then throughout the fair. Imagine it, a whole carnival filled with one song ringing from every single person. We felt so important that night to have started it all.

We became the seven seas. In our father's eyes we were perfect. He saw in us cool, clear water, sunlight shining through us like jewels after a storm, heard the sound of the waves against the shore and felt the quiet stillness of night. But our mother knew better. She knew what was to come, that the world would come and take from us what it wanted, leave us soiled and ruined if we weren't careful. "You have no idea yet what you are capable of, what is inside each and every one of you," she said, and she told us that although we were seven sisters we were unique, each with our own color and wind and breeze, that we could call forth ships and tie ourselves to the rhythms of the heavens. Like the seas, we had our own talents and gifts, ways that we could connect people or tear them apart. Some of us loved science, wanted to unlock the mysteries of the universe and find the cures to illness and pollution. Others preferred to cook, to combine ingredients, season them with salt and watch them bubble and warm. Some felt most alive when we were painting worlds into being, stretching our hands across piano keys, finding the perfect metaphor for the way the waves hammered the shore.

We wanted to be things: doctors and astronauts and painters and explorers. Our mother told us to dream. She would help us. She would pay for our schooling and send us to tutors and give us everything we needed to shape this world into the place we wanted it to be.

"You should not be pushing them like this," our father told her. "They are perfect already." But our mother told him that he did not know what it was like, to be seven women in this world. He did not know all the terrible things that could happen. "They do not need to be afraid," said our father. "I will protect them."

We became the seven wonders of the world. Our father whistled, and we fell in line, the oldest to the youngest, and we felt his pride. We stood in a row while people admired us, compared our noses and foreheads, noted which sister was the prettiest, which was the thinnest, which had the brightest curls. We tightened in our stomachs and stood tall and hoped they would choose us. Some preferred the sister who was built strong and sturdy, like the pyramids in Egypt, with powerful legs that kept her grounded in this world. Others chose the sister who was tall, willowy, natural as the hanging gardens, with long curly hair and eyes that blossomed when she smiled. Still others chose the two who stood as stiff as statues, who carved and shaped their bodies through exercise, the one adding mass to her muscles to make herself large, the other spending hours running on the beach to make her limbs long and lean. They wore low necklines and sleeveless shirts to show their chiseled muscles, and our father's friends smiled in approval. "They are all beautiful," our father would say when he showed us off, and his friends would shake their heads and say, "Yes, but oh, this one here, she is really something."

He asked us to sing, to show his friends everything we could do. We hated to perform, and sometimes we protested, but we loved to feel our father's pride. He sat his guests down, and we played quartets on stringed instruments and sang harmonies and brought out our best paintings for them to admire. One sister played the harp, and her music became a temple that pointed the audience to God. One wrote poems that immortalized loved ones, her words the stones that entombed and honored the departed. Perhaps the lighthouse sister was their favorite, though. The way she stood so tall and bright and sang warnings about the dangers that were to come.

We became the seven deadly sins. We didn't mean to be, but it happened. We all worked hard, fought for the kind of success we each wanted, but not all of us made it. Some were more beautiful. Some were smarter. Some more talented. We opened our mouths to sing and listened this time to the individual sounds that we made, some clearer, some higher. We stood in front of a mirror and lined ourselves up side-by-side to see ourselves the way our father's friends saw us. We saw then that some were prettier. Some would always shine brighter.

One sister starved herself. She could not make her body as thin as the others could and so she gave in to gluttony, ate all she could and then rid herself of it, again and again. She tied a string around her waist each morning, sucked in her breath until the ribs poked through her shirt. Her mind grew focused on this new goal, and she forgot all her old ones.

One sister stayed up late into the night studying. Some people called her ugly, but she had always been the smartest, and now she was determined to leave the others far behind. She would show the world what a girl was capable of, show it that a girl could cure illnesses and solve equations that would puzzle the smartest men. In her ambition and pride she forgot about her sisters, was even ashamed and embarrassed of some of us. She forgot how we used to sing together, how when our voices intertwined in harmonies no one could look away.

One sister bought new dresses every day. She was beautiful, the most beautiful of all, and she knew it. When she walked by, everyone stared and pointed. They followed her, worshipped her even. It wasn't enough, though. She gulped at the attention like it was air, water, food—greedily, hungrily. It became necessary. Without it, she could not survive.

One sister trained her body to run. She was fast. She won races all over the world, and she laughed at her sisters' obsession with beauty or brains. Her body would take her to the top, her long muscles and her powerful lungs. But one day she fell and broke her ankle and was told she would never run again. Her fury was magnificent. She raged at anyone who came near, was determined to find someone to blame. After that her wrath consumed her. She was no longer strong or fast or athletic. Only angry.

One sister despaired. She had wanted to be so many things, but she failed at them all. She could not run fast enough. She could not study hard enough. She could not make her body thin enough. She knew there was no point to the struggle, not when she was only one of seven talented and beautiful sisters. She became lazy, spent her days lying in the grass and watching the clouds, slept late into the morning and stayed up far into the night reading books that gave her nothing but pleasure. If she could not be what she wanted, she would not try.

One sister hated how easily success came to the other sisters and not to her. For her it was not enough to give up. If she could not have it, she did not want anyone to have it. Our mother warned her to rejoice at our successes, but she was blinded by envy. At night she cut off the other sisters' hair and tore their dresses, burned their books and pencils. She spread rumors, told our neighbors we had done terrible things so that they could not look at us the same way, never again see in us the seven innocent and pure sisters who had once united a carnival in song.

One sister found validation from anyone who would give it to her. She stayed out late each night trying to make men notice. She craved their attention and accepted it at any cost. She let them touch her and whisper lies into her ear, anything to make her feel loved and important again.

"My beautiful girls," said our mother. "What are you doing to yourselves?" It was not too late to keep the promise we had made to her so long ago. We were all bright and strong and capable, and the world was still our own, but we were starting to forget.

We became the seven continents, valleys and mountains and plains, long endless steppes and jungles and beaches, once bound together in a single mass, and now broken apart. One sister became Antarctica, cold and silent and inscrutable. One became the deserts of Africa, hot sun and priceless jewels that people would war over. One became Europe, ethereal and dark. One North America with its powerful trees and great lakes, and one South America, rainforests and colorful birds and bright blue beaches. One Australia, with beauty untouched and wild. One Asia, full of spice and mystery and mountains that could have led the people to heaven.

We were everything good in this world, and everything dangerous. And it stole from us the things it wanted. Like we were the land itself, the world pillaged and mined and destroyed. When we danced too boldly, it reached out and grabbed our bodies. When we opened our mouths to sing, it sang over us. When we offered our ideas, it had better ones, louder ones. We tried to be the things we had dreamt of becoming, but it was harder than our mother had said it would be.

One sister was too beautiful, and the world would not be satisfied without owning her. So it modeled and showcased her like she was an animal, made her resent the beauty that she had been given. One night men raped her again and again, and she returned to us damaged and cowering.

One sister was not beautiful enough, and the world had other uses for her. It would use her body to make strong sons, work her until she was haggard and old, because what harm was there in that when she was not beautiful to begin with?

One sister was too smart, held too many answers inside of her. But the world never learned to listen, never saw past her wild hair and too-bright eyes. And so it silenced her, yelled over her until she finally learned to stop talking.

One sister was too trusting. She believed what the world said, welcomed it into her home without skepticism or doubt and lived the way it told her to live. And after it misused and took advantage of her, she became tough and calloused, the most hardened of us all.

One sister was too strong, and the world feared her. She made it feel insecure. And so it found the thing that most made her powerful and alive and took that from her, left her lifeless and despairing and weak.

One sister was too quiet. She had important things to say and wonderful talents to share, but she did not want to fight to be noticed. The world assumed that meant she had nothing to give, and so it ignored and overlooked her.

One sister was too wild and could not be tamed. And so the world gave her a husband who beat her when she disobeyed him. One night he went too far. Her bones broke under his anger, and she came crawling back to us.

That was when we remembered the way we once ran over the hills when we were children, played in the colors of the rainbow and sang harmonies into the night. We knew then that our mother had been right all along in her caution and worry, but what was there to do about it anymore?

We became the seven daughters of Atlas. Our father joined our mother in her worry for us, and he walked the rest of his life with the terrible burden. We grew up. We were chased by important lovers, and we birthed important sons, men whose names would be remembered long after ours were forgotten. They founded cities and empires while our bodies were claimed and used and discarded. One man would not leave us alone. For years he pursued us, and we could do nothing to stop him. We heard stories about him, how he hunted animals to extinction, drank too much and attacked other women, raged about the earth preying on the most helpless and weak. Our father trembled for us. "How could I live if he ever found you?" he said. "I must protect you somehow, like I promised so long ago." He drew us back to himself, hid us away in the house of our childhood in hopes that he could turn back the clock, keep us young and innocent and safe.

But that was not enough. Our hunter chased us still. "You will never be safe while you are on this earth," said our father. "Not as seven sisters." He had another idea. He would turn us into stars and set us among the clouds. "And whenever I am lonely, I will look up and see my seven perfect daughters shining brightly." We begged him not to do it. We said that we loved this world. We would rather live in it and be damaged by it than to hide away forever in the heavens. We would grow stronger. We would learn to fight back. We would retrain our voices to sing and shout and lead the people in song. There was power in seven sisters, all one and all unique. If he gave us time, we would show him. But he said this was the only way. This was the way to be strong, strong enough to last through the generations. We would be remembered, worshipped, studied.

The night was cold and clear when he took us out onto the hill, the sky dark and waiting. There was new snow on the mountain. He hugged us goodbye and said he would remember us always. "Sailors will use you to find their way home, and children will sing songs about you, and every culture across the world will make up legends of your origins, and I will know that you are protected." And so one by one, he lit us on fire and flung us into the heavens, high above the earth, and there we burned, forever safe and separate and silent. We are there still, and from our place in the sky we look down upon the earth that once belonged to us, the continents shifting and shaking, the rivers carving new valleys and canyons, the wind keening, the snow falling, the oceans rising, the ponderosas growing straight and strong on the hills.

SNOW GLOBE

Two towns over, a twelve-year-old is admitted to the hospital with a snow globe buried in her vagina. Curiosity? Experimentation? Abuse? Inside the globe a plastic princess stands outside a castle— frosty blue gown, long golden hair, clouds of glitter floating above her head. Inside the x-ray machine, the girl moans, and the doctors shake their heads at all the things they have seen.

Here in our town, I prep for your birthday party. You are turning seven, and you love robots as much as other girls love princesses. It doesn't matter to me. Doesn't matter that you dirtied the Cinderella rug I put in your room, the one I would have treasured as a child, tore the arms off of the beautiful dolls I gave you and built monsters, ripped holes in the knees of your ballerina tights playing football with your brothers. I know that parenting is acceptance, and I will let you be anyone you want to be.

Two towns over, the twelve-year-old's mother sobs. We will read about it in the paper next week. "What a strange world," your father will say, and I will nod because it's what I've always said too. The girl's mother clutches her daughter's hand and asks what happened. What possibly could have possessed her? She lists the good things she has done for her daughter, stacks them up against the act that landed them in the emergency room, tries to understand, as if parenting is a scale, as if, say, it didn't matter that my own mother was stoned for my seventh birthday because at least she was sober for my sixth and eighth. She smoothes her daughter's hair off of her forehead and tells her they will get through this, together, but the girl turns away.

Here in our town, you blow out your candles. I have made you a robot cake, cut it into squares and rectangles, frosted robot arms and legs, and your eyes shine like Cinderella's when you see it. There is no scale in your life, no balance of good and bad. You, my darling, are my world. Your happiness is my own. Your childhood, my purpose. At your birthday party, your friends dance around you. They hit red and blue balloons into the air and jump on the furniture to keep the balloons off the ground. The whole room bubbles with primary colors and laughter and children. If I'd had a mother who loved me like I love you, I would have asked for pink and purple and white, but you refused when I tried to convince you, wrinkled your nose and made a gagging sound, and so I rumpled your hair and laughed in a way that said, "I don't understand you, but I will give you what you want" and returned the streamers and glitter that could have turned our whole house into a castle, your childhood into the fairytale I wish it could be. Parenting is acceptance, and nurturing, and love no matter what. A pillow on the couch tears open, but I do not hit anyone, do not even yell. Your brothers break out of their bedroom where they have been told to play video games until the party is over. You and your friends squeal, and soon the house has turned into a game of chase, cops versus robbers, boys versus girls. I watch you, and I wish you could know, and am glad that you don't, how very happy you are.

Two towns over, the girl's father joins his family at the hospital, and the girl looks away. Imagine the embarrassment, your father knowing you've done something like that. Unless of course your father were to blame, which he must have been, somehow. The father puts his hand on the girl's arm, and she shrinks away, or maybe I only imagine she shrinks away, imagine it because this is something I know that I pray you never learn, how fathers can turn on their children while their wives are passed out in the next bedroom, do things that their daughters will try to forget for the rest of their lives. "Excuse me," the doctor says. "Could we see you outside for a minute? We have a few questions." So the father leaves his daughter, but before he does, he leans down and kisses the top of her head.

Here in our town, you are opening your birthday presents. Your friends have given you everything a little girl could ever want—art sets and Barbie dolls and Playmobile castles. They are children and do not know you like I know you. You open a Cinderella snow globe, a carriage carrying a princess off to her very first ball, and you tilt it upside down, and your friends gasp when Cinderella's carriage fills with glitter. You tap at the globe like you wish you could get inside it, take it all apart and see how it fits together. Then you set it down. You are more interested in the basketball your father has given you. You call your friends outside to practice shooting into the hoop we have lowered so that you can reach it. You dash around the driveway, knocking opponents aside and throwing the ball into the air. When you can't make the shot, your father lifts you on his shoulders, and up there you look to me like royalty, dropping the basketball into the hoop and raising your arms and cheering. The sun shines down on your golden ponytail, and through the clouds the light sparkles like the glitter in a snow globe.

Two towns over, a social worker is called in. She will be the girl's fairy godmother, turn the rats into snow-white steeds, moldy pumpkins into carved carriages. The questions she will ask the girl and her parents will be painful—embarrassing, but necessary. The girl will resent it, but if I could talk to her I would tell her that Cinderella will never escape her evil stepmother without the fairy godmother, that she will spend her whole girlhood trying to find food when her mother comes home drunk, hiding the money she makes in high school, sleeping in the park when her father is home. "Accept the help," I would tell her. "Be grateful. Your life could still become something wonderful."

Here in our town, your father is putting you to bed. I have bathed you, and now I read to your brothers while your father tucks you in. You are overtired from your party, crying at everything that does not go your way. You stand on the bathroom stool in a football jersey that fits you like a ball gown, and your father brushes your teeth gently, the way I have taught him, and then reads you a bedtime story, and you are laughing and fussing, emotions intertwined as tightly as they can be only in childhood. The wind is blowing hard outside. This winter will be a cold one. I kiss your brothers goodnight and tiptoe down the hall to your room. I press my ear to the closed door, listening, ready, just in case. Your father is trying to make you laugh, and he tickles you. You giggle, but then you scream at him to stop, and my hand is on the doorknob in a second, almost turning, but instead I wait.

I hold my breath.

I strain and listen, listen for something, for everything.

I hear your father whisper apologies, sing you a song, kiss your forehead. He switches off the light, and I sneak away.

Two towns over, the doctor taps on the girl's door. She sits alone in her hospital bed and does not look up. He hands her the snow globe, sterilized now, and sparkling. "Maybe you want this back?" he asks, and she takes it, but says nothing. He pauses before he leaves, pauses to say something, something that could make sense of everything, make it all better, but he is a medical doctor and knows best how to fix bodies, and so he puts his hand on the girl's shoulder for a moment and then leaves. When the doctor is gone the girl tilts the globe upside down. She watches the snow fall, and she remembers the year before, when her teacher took the class to hear the symphony. The cellos painted the hall the color of the night sky, and the drums crashed above her head like bursts of stars, and then the violins began to play, and they turned the atrium into a globe filled with glitter and light, the girl inside it a princess, or a fairy, or a queen.

AERIAL SPRAY

A little boy stands at his window in Scooby Doo pajamas and wet hair. He touches his fingers to the glass and feels the Texas summer hot against his skin. Downstairs his parents yell at each other, and tomorrow his father will move out, but in his hand tonight he clutches his first tooth, small and white and sharp, and he waits.

Tonight the tooth fairy will die, under a spray of chemicals sent to end the West Nile Virus.

If he had only lost his tooth last spring, had let his father yank it out when he offered, but he didn't and this summer in Texas the West Nile Virus spread like a dust storm and a little girl died in a hospital bed and the city said that enough was enough, something had to be done. Protestors said there were other ways, but the city asked how many people had to die. They filled the sky with shining lights and helicopters that rained chemicals down over the streets, and they told the children to stay inside and shut their windows until the aerial spray was over. They must have forgotten about the fairies.

The little boy knows the tooth fairy will try to come. She will ignore the city warnings and will fly through the aerial spray to reach him, like she has flown every night to reach children. And she will die. The little boy knows she will die. He sees her struggling against the chemicals that cling like lead to her wings and fill her lungs. He sees her coughing, sputtering. A plate shatters downstairs. The little boy's fist tightens around the tooth and a drop of blood appears on his palm.

Tomorrow he will search the woods for the tooth fairy. His mother will dress him in long sleeves and gloves to keep the chemicals from his skin. She will look relieved to send him out to play and will tell him to stay as long as he wants. She will say she is sure the tooth fairy is not dead, only distracted, but the little boy will know better. The woods will be silent, and the little boy will look under rocks and logs for trails of golden fairy dust, but he will find nothing but dead frogs and insects. He will build a fairy house in case the tooth fairy really is alive and needs a place to rest. He will rinse the house in the creek to wash the poison from it and will carpet it with pine needles and build a bed of twigs. He will hang curtains made of leaves from the windows to shelter the house in case the helicopters come again with their aerial spray.

Tonight, though, the little boy waits in his bedroom. He whispers to the tooth fairy not to come, but he knows he is too late. He stands at his window and listens.

Listens to the yelling.

Listens to the poison rain.

Listens to the fairy wings that beat, gentle and faint.

ALSO LONELY,
ALTHOUGH ON LAND

All night long on the island the lights of salsa clubs shine across deserted beaches. The music pulses. The breezes blow. The dancers breathe in salt, slide their feet across the sandy floor, arms and legs sticky with sweat. Stella is among them, but she moves away from the other dancers, pulled or pushed by something she can't explain. Only a cement ledge and a velvet rope separate the club from the beach, and Stella slides under the rope and drops to the sand.

The beach is busy during the day, but now it's quiet, deserted. The waves roll black against the night. Stella walks to the edge of the water and listens to the ocean, the music from the club low in the background. There are no stars tonight. The moon is small and pale. Stella sits down on the sand, takes her shoes off and puts her feet in the foam.

The moonlight catches an object on the shore, sends the reflection shining above the sand like a beacon. Stella walks to it. It's only a beer bottle. The beach is littered with them. She picks it up, intending to carry it back with her and throw it away. Inside, though, she sees something—a piece of paper, perhaps, an old receipt, a napkin—and the bottle is capped. Stella uncorks it and reaches in. She pulls out the paper and unfolds it. On the paper is a message, like Columbus used to report his discoveries to the Queen of Castile, like the Zeppelin L

19 crew threw into the North Sea when they knew they were doomed. The message Stella finds reads: "Lost at sea. Very lonely. Looking for company and friendship. Please reply."

It sounds like a want ad in the paper, Stella thinks. Do people still write those, or is it all through Craigslist now, or dating apps on phones? She smiles and remembers being young, in college and on vacation, that feeling that nothing from home could touch her there and nothing on vacation could follow her home. The message is surely a practical joke from one of the island's vacationers, some young person playing pranks with the ocean, casting a line and seeing what will turn up. Stella slips the message into the pocket of her shorts, throws the bottle away in a trashcan near the club, and returns to the music, the dance.

Stella's husband waits for her inside. "Where were you?" he asks. "I've been worried." His shirt is discolored with sweat. It clings to his body, the middle-aged sag of his chest, the roundness of his belly.

"I just had to get some air," Stella says, and she tells him she's tired, ready to go to bed.

"Once upon a time you could dance all night," says Jimmy.

"Once upon a time I was younger," she says.

They were here once before, here on this warm beach with its jungles and salsa music, back when they were in college, their relationship new and frenzied. So much had happened since then, decades of life. That was before their daughters were born and demanded their attention and resources, before they stopped talking to each other, telling each other the small and insignificant parts of their days, before Jimmy's affair with his coworker, a powerful woman who wore heels and pencil skirts like battle armor, whose very demeanor made Stella feel made of lace. Now they've returned to see if they can recreate what they had back then, if they can stay out all night and match their bodies to each other, wake in the morning and pick up where they left off, walk through parrot-filled jungles and skinny dip in dark nighttime oceans, fall in love again with the earth, with each other.

Stella wakes up hungover. She and Jimmy spend the morning in their hotel room. Before their room was cheap and smelly, something no one past thirty would stay in. This time it's big and clean, white sheets, air conditioning, room service. They order breakfast brought up to them and they read while they eat. Today they will walk through the jungle to find one of their favorite beaches from before, a quiet little cove with tall dangerous waves that only the locals visit. When they were here before they snuck out of their hotel room and crept through the jungle at night to reach the deserted beach, their bodies tingling in the heat, the waves—as they crashed against sharp rocks— pulling them deeper in love.

This time on their walk through the jungle they slap at mosquitoes and wipe sweat from their foreheads. Jimmy rubs sunscreen into Stella's shoulders, and it mixes with sand and scrapes against her burnt skin. They sit on beach towels and watch surfers paddle their boards far out to where the most dangerous waves crash. Local children splash naked on the shore. Stella thinks of the message in the bottle. Someone sent it, even if it was just a joke. Someone who was lonely. It could have been anyone. It could be someone here on this island, someone she could meet. Jimmy leans over and kisses Stella's shoulder.

"Ow," says Stella.

"Remember last time we were here?" says Jimmy.

Of course she remembers. It was cold on the beach that night, and he held her, and she told him things she'd never told anyone, the secrets of her life, the childhood traumas, the loneliness, the mother who left her while she was still a girl, the little sister she raised alone, how she too had left, drawn to a boy who could give her things Stella never could. She told Jimmy how she'd never had friends, always thought before him that the safest way to live was without other people. It felt like waking up, telling him all these things. It felt like healing, total and complete, like after such intimacy they would last forever.

"Let's not go back," says Jimmy, and Stella stops rubbing on sunscreen and turns to him. Back home their world is dull and muted, but here, Jimmy says, here there are blazing sunsets, sunrises that light symphonies into the sky each morning, dark coffee grown in the fields just outside of town, emerald and sapphire birds winging through the clouds, fiery volcanoes ready to explode.

Jimmy says, "Maybe not here, nearby, a city where we can find jobs, close enough to come here often, far enough from our old life. Our girls will be in college soon. They could spend their holidays here. A new start."

"Just think about it," he says, and a breeze blows through the trees, makes the ocean beyond shimmer and dance.

It was nearly two years ago, the affair. "How much of a cliché can you be?" Stella had yelled after he told her. He promised it was over. He would do what he needed to repair his marriage: counseling, retreats, workbooks. Stella blames herself, though, because her whole life, people have been leaving. It is as if she were born to be left, a magnet facing the wrong way. Her body chants it with each heartbeat: "Everyone you love will leave." Even here on the island the waves pulse this truth to her, the breeze carries it. Jimmy came back, but she wonders if he will stay.

That night they have dinner at a beachfront restaurant, where they eat freshly caught fish cleaned and cooked right in front of them and watch the sun drop into the ocean. They walk together along the shore. Jimmy holds Stella's hand, and her long skirt drags in the water. Her hair, damp in the humid air, tickles her shoulders. Jimmy reminds her of their last time on this shore, when they were only nineteen and spent their days catching waves, laughing and splashing, their pasts at last starting to feel in the past, their futures bright and large. It was also here where she found the message the night before. She doesn't have it with her, but she's memorized what it says, and she recites it to herself while she walks with Jimmy. She glances across the beach, tries to figure out which vacationer wrote it, who is here looking for someone else.

They have children, Jimmy and Stella, two not-little-enough girls with long blond hair and dark brown eyes who will be leaving for college soon, and those two are Stella's world, but she is not theirs. Once upon a time she was. Once upon a time her face was the only thing they saw, all it took for smiles to light in their eyes. But then there was kindergarten, and friends, and new teachers, and the world became bigger and their mother shrank. Stella tries hard not to resent them for the way they no longer need her, the way they too will soon leave.

The next day Stella and Jimmy rent snorkeling equipment and swim through coral reefs to look at fish. It takes Stella a few minutes to learn how to breathe through the snorkel, how every breath must be measured and deep, but once she does she could swim for hours without lifting her head. Stella and Jimmy are both strong swimmers, but the reef they want to snorkel in—still bright and pristine—is far from the shore, and they must swim over half a mile across open water. They hold hands so they will not become separated, and the waves push and pull at them, but neither lets go.

At the reef the water is still, but they continue to hold hands. With their free arms they propel themselves along the surface, watch the fish through their diving masks, listen to the rhythm of their breath through the tubes loud in their ears. The fish do not notice them, and they swim without fear—ruby and cobalt, fire orange and absinthe green, striped and spotted and ringed. Stella reaches out and touches a bright yellow one. When she smiles, bubbles from her lungs leak into the water. She wishes her daughters could be here swimming beside her, the whole family together in this moment of magic. Soon, she thinks. Maybe. Jimmy sticks his leg out and touches hers, and she laughs at the way his big toe tickles the inside of her knee. This is something they didn't do last time they were here, the cost to rent fins and snorkels more than they could spare on a college-student budget.

Jimmy points far below the surface to a deeper darker place where a school of lime-colored fish swim. He looks at her and nods, and then releases her hand. He holds his breath and swims down into the ocean, down where it is too dark for Stella to see him. He disappears, and Stella imagines he is being pulled under and away by a current or some mysterious force far beneath the surface, the deep calling him away from her, the way, she thinks, she's always known it would. She is both devastated and relieved, that what she knew would happen has happened.

A moment later, though, she sees bubbles, and Jimmy is behind them, returned from the dark cave he was exploring, smiling at her through his mask. He reaches out to take her hand again, but she swims away.

It's then she sees it, something caught beneath the coral. It looks like a piece of trash or a bottle, and she holds her breath and swims down to pick it up. It's just like the bottle she found on the beach the other night, corked with a strip of paper inside. Jimmy swims over to her and reaches out to take it, but she clutches it to her chest, keeps it for herself.

They swim back separately, although Jimmy reaches out to touch her every now and then, to make sure she hasn't drifted too far away. When they are back on shore they return their snorkeling equipment and Jimmy asks if she's going to throw the bottle away. Stella clutches it and says no, she'll keep it for a little while.

When Stella is at last alone, she reads the message: "Still lost at sea. Still lonely. Waiting for your reply."

Stella sits in the sand and reads the note again and again. She doesn't know who or what it's from, but she loves the way it makes her feel, more alive, like she's keeping a secret that's both dangerous and innocent.

That night while Jimmy is sleeping Stella slips away. The moon shines across the beach, and Stella dumps a bottle of Cola into the sand. She pulls a pen and piece of notebook paper from her purse. On the paper she writes: "Dear Lost at Sea, I'm also lonely, although on land. You can talk to me." She rolls the paper up tight, slips it into the bottle and screws on the lid, throws it into the ocean.

In the afternoon they catch a taxi into the city and spend the afternoon wandering neighborhoods. They build their fantasy escape life, dream of which homes they would live in, which schools their daughters would attend, which cafes they would frequent. Their hair is stiff from the ocean, and their skin still smells of sunshine and salt. Jimmy buries his nose in Stella's neck and breathes. "If we lived here, you would always smell this way," he says.

This is better than pencil skirts and Chanel No. 5, Stella thinks, but she does not say. She thinks of the message she sent last night, wonders how or when or where she can expect a reply.

It comes that night, when she and Jimmy are finishing dinner. They've made sandwiches to eat by the ocean, and a bottle washes to shore, right to the place where they are sitting, and Stella runs through the water to it.

"Another one?" asks Jimmy.

"Strange," says Stella. Jimmy offers to take their trash away, and while he is gone Stella reads the note:

"The ocean is full of creatures stranger than you could imagine, but there is no one like me. Do you know how that feels? I am glad to have found you."

Before Jimmy returns Stella scribbles a reply, slips it into the bottle pushes the cork in, offers the message back to the sea:

"Here on land it's also crowded. People talk, and they say nothing. Their bodies bump against each other in crowded dance halls, but they don't—can't—know if the person they've just touched is happy or terribly sad. All we know to do is pretend."

She wakes up early, the sky still dark, only the faintest hint of dawn lighting the horizon above the ocean. She leaves Jimmy sleeping. A message waits for her on the beach:

"You don't need to pretend with me. Tell me everything you want someone to know."

So Stella sits on the sand, with her notebook and a pencil. The words come fast and easy, everything she hasn't said, everything she's wanted to.

"Dear Lost at Sea," she writes: "I am always being left, by my mother and my sister and my husband. Even now the gulls fly away from me, not toward, and the tide is going out, pulling the water away, carrying the sea creatures away with it. I do not know how to make myself enough for someone to stay. Jimmy came back, but I know he will not leave again. His affair is over, but it will never really be, and soon my children will be gone too. I am afraid of the moment I am at last all alone."

She sits there on the sand until the sun has risen, and when at last her letter is complete, she sends it into the waves.

Jimmy is awake when she returns, and wants to know where she was.

"Nowhere," she says. She tells him she wanted to see morning begin on the beach, wanted to see the gulls and herons fly through the sunrise.

"I wish I could have seen it too," says Jimmy. "It sounds magical." He leans in to kiss her, but she tells him she needs to shower.

She keeps watch all day, while she and Jimmy travel around the island, sit on one beach, eat lunch on another. Jimmy asks what she's looking for, why she seems more distracted than she was before, and she tells him to stop imagining things. It gives her a little spike of joy, or maybe spite, or some combination, that she has a secret now, that she is the one telling the lies.

That night the dance halls are filled with bubbles. They float through the open doorways and out across the beaches, blow over the ocean. There is party ship out there, far away. Its lights shine red and green and blue on the water, and the music drifts to shore. Something jumps from the water, something large, although Stella can't see what it is in the darkness. Jimmy wanted to go out, return to the clubs and dance under the bubbles and lights, but Stella told him she was too tired, that she'd rather go to bed, but he should go and have a good time, she'd be fine.

Once alone she slipped away, headed to the deserted beach. Now she walks along the shore, her feet ankle-deep in the ocean, that shallow part where footprints disappear to the waves in an instant, and she scans the water for a bottle.

When she finds it the message reads: "Thank you for all you told me. I feel like I know you now. Here are some things about me: I love the smell of fireworks burning against the sky, the way the ocean stretches on and on and then drops off at the end of the world—have you ever seen this?—the sound of birds calling the sun to wake up each morning. I feel most alive when I have someone to love, but I am often afraid. Do you know what this is like too?"

Stella smiles while she reads the note. She breathes in the night, imagines the ocean falling off the end of the world in a giant waterfall, the sun a glowing sphere above it. She wishes she could spend all night on the beach, stay awake for hours sending messages through the waves.

"You've been lying to me," says Jimmy when Stella returns.

She's sorry she didn't make it back before he did, but she almost laughs at the accusation, the way it comes from him.

"You've been seeing someone," he says. "Or talking. Tell me who."

"I haven't," she says. "It's no one."

"I know it's someone," he says. "Please don't lie to me."

"So what if I am lying?" she says.

"Please don't," he says.

"It's nothing," she says. "No one." Then she smiles at him and a thought flashes across her mind. "Just a mermaid," she says.

Maybe she's spent too many years in the company of her little girls, but she imagines her new friend a mermaid after that, and she spends every minute she can on the beach sending letters back and forth. She hopes that one day they will meet, but even if they don't, it is still worth something, to feel so understood, the way she felt once upon a time with Jimmy. Jimmy walks with her when he can, but she finds excuses to slip away. "Where do you go?" he asks. His voice is filled with guilt, more than she heard two years ago, like now he finally understands. "We were having such a good time," he reminds her, and she says, "Yes, we were."

She leaves him in the mornings, buys bananas and milk from vendors, sips the blended drink through a straw. At night she watches the lights from the clubs, the lights that shine across the ocean, the way the sunset looks both the same and different each time, the way the ocean bursts into flames for a moment and then swallows the sun whole. And all the time she keeps watch, ready for the bottle that will bring her new message, ready to slide her reply into it, to throw it back to the water. Her flight back home approaches, her flight back to her old life with Jimmy, and he no longer mentions staying on the island, has given up that fantasy.

She talks to the mermaid about her mother.
She talks to the mermaid about her sister.
She talks to the mermaid about Jimmy, his affair.
She talks to the mermaid about her daughters.
The mermaid answers. She understands. She says things like, "That must have been terrible." "You are so strong." "I can't believe he treated you that way." "You deserve to feel loved."

Stella reads her notes, one by one. She sits by the water and polishes seashells between her fingers, and they shimmer silvery pink. Gulls encircle her now, eat the crumbs of her sandwich, come nearer and nearer. Everything around her sparkles and shines and seems to shout, you are home.

The morning of the flight Jimmy's suitcases are packed and waiting by the door. "When we get home I think we need to see a marriage counselor again," he says. He says he was foolish to believe their problems wouldn't follow them to the island. He tells Stella to hurry and pack her bag; the taxi will be here soon.

"I'm not coming," Stella says.

"What do you mean?" he asks, so she tells him she wants to stay on the island, like they talked about.

"We were only dreaming," he says. "I thought you knew it wasn't real."

She tells him whether it was a dream or not, she's made up her mind.

"Is it the mermaid?" he asks. "Whoever that is," and Stella does not answer. Soon her daughters will leave home and go to college. Jimmy might find another woman, or he might not, but she'll never really know for sure again. But this new friend, this stranger lost at sea who writes to her through saltwater-drenched messages, whoever she is and whatever form she takes, she will be there.

"You're acting crazy," says Jimmy. "You're acting like a child."

"I made up my mind days ago," says Stella. "You can't change it."

"If you stay," says Jimmy. "That's it. You'll be the one who left, left our whole family."

"It's about time," she says.

Stella goes back to the beach. She sits down by the ocean and watches everything slip away. The waves pull at the sand beneath her feet, and the moon pulls at the ocean, everything all around her, disappearing, drawn away from her, but also toward. The sun is high and bright, but soon it will set, and night will fall across the water again.

She holds a slip of paper, scribbles a note: "Dear Lost at Sea, Jimmy has gone, but I am here still, although on land. I have never left anyone before, have only been left, but now I am leaving, because I am staying here with you. We may never meet, and that is okay, because we will keep talking through the ocean, and we will no longer be lonely, or lost."

FRONTERA SECA

In Odessa the protestors line the streets, sun rising hot and bright behind them. They are oil field workers and businessmen, landmen and lawyers, babies in diapers, holding signs they are too small to lift, words they are too young to read.

Danny and his father fight their way through the traffic to join the other day laborers under the pavilions. They gather there every morning, thermoses filled with coffee, to wait for work, swap stories of their children, the families they've left behind, the new ones they've made.

"It can't be true," says one.

"Of course not," says another.

"But who knows," says a third.

There is a rumor, all anyone can talk about, not twenty-four hours old, as sudden and surprising as the West Texas wind that stirs up dust storms and rolls tumbleweeds across the desert. When the Rio Grande is dry, the rumor says, the international border will be dissolved. There will be no more separation.

"It is almost gone," Danny says to his father Juan Ramón. "The Río Bravo." Danny is just a boy, not yet sixteen. He speaks to his father in Spanish, although his English is strong enough that he could make it through high school, even go on to college if the risk weren't too great. He hasn't been to the river since he and his father crossed it three years ago, but it's never left his thoughts, that line that determines there and here.

He was twelve when they crossed, still a child but old enough to work. He left behind his mother Carolina and brother Benigno and a baby sister María Fernanda. His father promised he would send for them once he and Danny worked for a few years and earned money and legal visas. Since then they've scraped up just enough money to send down to Mexico, just enough to keep Beni and Marifer in school, to offer them a better childhood than the one Danny had, but not enough to bring them up here.

"It's only a rumor, son," says Juan Ramón. "Neither side would sign such a treaty."

"Why not?" asks Danny.

Juan Ramón reminds Danny of all the people who want to keep them out, all the fear that would accompany an open border, that accompanies even a closed one.

"I know," says Danny, "But the world is changing. It already has."

Juan Ramón laughs at this, at his son's ability to hope, but then again, once the Rio Bravo roared through northern Mexico and kept his forefathers alive; now it's only a weak trickle that snakes through the desert.

"Just don't get your hopes up," he says.

Beyond their pavilion the town is a madhouse of hope and fear and noise. A church marquee on the corner reads, "OUR GOD IS A GOD OF ORDER. PRAY FOR RAIN." Environmentalists pass out flyers asking for donations, listing steps to save the river. They have been talking for years, and no one listened until now.

At the intersection downtown a congregation from one of the town's churches has gathered to pass out tracts. "God causes it to rain on the just and on the unjust," the pastor shouts, "but this treaty is unjust." The crowd claps and the pastor continues. "Join us here every Saturday morning to pray publically for rain, just like the prophet Elijah. God will show his power."

The day Danny and his father left Mexico, they went to the bus station together, where Juan Ramón counted out bills and coins and asked for two tickets to Nuevo León. He and Danny would ride the bus and then walk from there. In the bus station a mother and her three children sat on the floor sleeping in dusty clothes, their backs against the tiled wall. When the woman saw Danny looking at her children she nudged her daughter over to Danny. The little girl put a sticker on Danny's hand, and he shook it off so that he didn't have to pay for it. "I'm sorry," he told her, and hoped she understood he had no money either.

Benigno kicked a rock around the station, and Danny kicked it back to him a couple times. Beni was nine then, and Danny's best friend. He wore Danny's hand-me-down sweatshirt and combed his hair like Danny's. Marifer was just learning to walk. She stumbled around the bus terminal grabbing onto chairs and smiling at other passengers. Danny and Beni tossed her back and forth between one another, and their mother yelled to them to be careful. When the bus driver called for the tickets, Juan Ramón put his hand on Danny's shoulder and pointed him toward the bus.

His mother kissed his head. "Help your papá and remember to pray," she said.

Now Beni attends the preparatoria, the first in Danny's family to make it past eighth grade. Marifer is in prescholar. On that day before he boarded the bus Danny hugged her and Beni and said he would see them soon. "Will you still remember Spanish?" Beni asked him, and Danny said of course he would.

"I don't want to wait," Danny says to his father now under the pavilion.

"What for what?"

"For the river to disappear," he says. "For the border to be gone. I want to do something."

His father waits, and Danny explains. "It's so small. What if we helped to make it smaller? Dried it out or something?"

"You're crazy," says Juan Ramón. Even if the rumor were true, he tells his son, the river can't be dried so easily. It's weak out in West

Texas, but stronger in other places. Besides, he reminds Danny, it's too big a risk, with their forged documents.

"You will see your brother again," Juan Ramón says. "If we work hard enough."

"That's not enough," says Danny. "We need to do more." Juan Ramón asks what he has in mind, and Danny knows his father is only humoring him, but he mentions the many things that are already drying the river, things he's heard the environmentalists talk about for years—the dams and tributaries, the droughts and plants, the overuse from both Mexico and the United States. "Maybe we plant some weeds that will dry the river, or we build a dam here, where the river is already so small."

"I'm sorry, son," says Juan Ramón. "We've risked too much already. We can't throw that away."

The desert stars are smeared bright against the sky that night when Danny sneaks out of his house, grabs the keys to his father's truck, a map of Texas that will take him back to the Rio Grande. He feels the river calling to him, begging him to come home. He has friends here, loves cheeseburgers and football more than his father ever will. But he remembers waking up in the mornings with his brother sleeping next to him, Beni's breath fast and hot. He remembers the way the highland mountain air smelled, like baking bread and car exhaust and frying tortillas, how the church bells sang, and the buses sputtered down the streets, and shopkeepers splashed soapy water across the sidewalks and swept it away with a broom. He cannot live like this any more, torn between this place and that.

He slips his father's key into the ignition, and the motor coughs awake.

"Wait," he hears. His father is pounding the window, opening the passenger door, climbing inside. He yells at Danny inside the cab. "Where do you think you're going?" he asks.

"I'm sorry, Papá," Danny says. "You are too afraid, but I'm not, and I believe the rumor is true."

Juan Ramón puts his hand on his son's shoulder. "I'm glad you're not afraid," he says, and he tells Danny of his own fear, the way when they were crossing the river with other refugees he held his breath against any sound—every cry or cough or gasp for air—that could alert border patrol, the way he believed, back when they lived in the mountains of Mexico, that El Norte was the promised land, that everything would be easy once they crossed the river.

Danny waits, doesn't answer right at once. Then he says, "The rumor is true, Papá. I know it, even if you do not." He shifts the truck into drive. "You cannot stop me from going. You can come if you want to."

Danny and Juan Ramón drive hours through the desert, under the cover of night. They dodge rabbits that grow daring and run across the road. A white owl swoops low in front of their truck. They carry their forged documents and hope, as they always hope, that if they are pulled over the officers will not look too closely. When the river is dry these documents will not matter, Danny thinks, and without the added cost of paperwork and coyotes and bribes, they will be able to afford to bring their family to Texas safely. "I know what we are risking," he says. "I know what we risked back then too."

They had stopped at a hardware store on the way out of town, bought bag after bag of sand, tarps, plants. Danny had everything planned out, and his father shook his head at the money he was spending but did not stop him. Danny sees in his father's eyes sometimes the guilt, that of all his children, Danny was the one who had to sacrifice, that now Marifer and Beni go to school and live normal childhoods in Mexico while Danny does not. He knows that this is the reason his father is indulging him now, an act of love, of remorse, and not of hope.

In his lap Danny carries a rosary and a few prayer candles. "I think Mamá would want us to pray," he says. They listen to the local radio stations, normally quiet by this time, but tonight loud and full of speculations about the rumor of the dry border. Pro-border terrorists have been arrested trying to open the Elephant Butte Dam in New

Mexico to refill the river, a newscaster reports. Radio preachers warn against the antichrist's arrival when all nations are one day united. Environmentalists list steps to ensure the river's survival. Economists and anthropologists debate what would happen financially and culturally if the two countries were to merge. It would be our destruction, say some. It would be our salvation, say others.

It's nearly dawn by the time they reach the river, only a few hours of darkness left for their work. They pick a spot that seems secluded, sit in the truck for a moment and listen to the howl of a Western Screech-Owl. "Are you sure?" Juan Ramón whispers. Danny nods and opens the door. The moon is small tonight, but the Texas stars light the river and turn the desert brush around it yellow. Danny walks toward the river, the river he has not seen in three years. He reaches down and touches the trickle of water, rolls his pants up and steps in. The water curls around his ankles, his toes sink in the sand. He stares into Mexico and wades deeper into the river until he stands in the middle. The water only reaches his shins, the river almost dry. He stretches out his hands, one to Texas, one to Mexico.

"Come on, son," his father calls, and he reminds Danny that the sun will rise soon.

Together they carry the sandbags from the truck and set them on the bank. The water is only a few feet wide here. Their task will be small. They work silently, laying the sandbags one on top of the each other in the river. Once a pair of headlights shine on the distant hills. They crouch low in the river, although there's nothing they can do to hide their truck, and they pray the headlights will not come nearer. "If we are caught, I'm sorry," Danny says. He slaps at insects. Overhead a pair of nighthawks circle as if watching. Their wings flash white as they swoop through the sky. Juan Ramón stands knee deep in the water and stacks the sand. The river hits the sand, slows, rises. They keep building. This dam is all that Danny can do right now to see his family. Build this dam and hope that God recognizes it.

"What would you do if they came here?" Danny asks his father.

"I would take Beni to the high school and show him the auditorium where he would graduate. Someday I know I will see him cross the stage there." Juan Ramón pauses a moment. "I'm sorry you could not finish school."

"I know," says Danny. "Maybe someday."

He listens to the desert night, quiet but for the whistling killdeer, so different from the place he was born. He remembers it well, the way nights in Mexico are almost as loud as the days, the way the neighbors watch TV on full volume and dogs bark and banda music plays until the gas trucks trumpet at dawn. When he first moved to Texas Danny could not sleep. His father held him tight and said everything would be fine, but Danny could not breathe in the silence of the West Texas nights.

There are parts of Texas he's come to love, though, the barbeque and the desert and the sprawling one-story houses that spill across the land. He thinks of his coworkers who have become like brothers, and he thinks of the friends he left behind in Mexico, the crowd of children who would gather in the evenings to kick a soccer ball around the street. He builds the dam and hopes that the dry river means he will no longer have to choose.

The last bag is in the river. Danny wades in and joins his father. They straighten the sandbags, make them even and tall. If God sees, he will know that they did their best, he will see what this means to them. Already the river's flow has stilled. Juan Ramón puts his hand on his son's shoulder. They do not speak, listen instead to the sound of the pool filling. In it Danny hears his mother's voice calling to him. He hears the noisy Mexican streets and the still Texas nights. He smells taco stands and barbeque joints, his old home and his new. He dips his hand in the water once more.

His father turns to leave. "Wait," Danny says. He says that he wants to pray. He says his mother would want them to pray. He takes the prayer candles from the truck and sets them in the sand. He fingers his rosary. Juan Ramón joins him but looks reluctant.

"Hijo," he says. "We need to go." Danny says it will not be long. Danny lights the candles, takes out a photo of his brother and sister, old and faded. He fingers his rosary and recites the Ave María, just as his mother taught him when he was a boy. "Dios te salve, María, llena eres de gracia." Juan Ramón shakes his head a little bit and smiles at his son, the way he still believes, at least for tonight. He joins in. "El Señor es contigo." The light from the candles flickers in the darkness, sparks rising into the desert sky.

Three hours south a group of refugees struggle through the desert, thirsty and tired, the water towers that would have saved their lives shot open by border patrol, spilled across the sand. Along the borders children Beni and Marifer's age are kept shivering in cages. In the Texas capital speechwriters are already updating campaign speeches to address environmental concerns, add promises of river preservation to their candidates' platforms. In the Odessa high schools the students will take sides, and teachers will wonder, although they're not allowed to ask, which are undocumented, which ones could disappear any day, sent back to the lives they ran away from. And down in Mexico, Beni and is waking up, combing his hair the way he remembers his brother combing his, putting on his school uniform, thinking of his brother and father. Some day he will see them again. He's sure.

"Santa María, Madre de Dios, ruega por nosotros, pecadores," Danny and his father recite together, the boy's eyes closed, his father's wide open to check for headlights on the horizon. "Ahora y en la hora de nuestra muerte, Amén." They make the sign of the cross and watch the candles burn. The Rio Grande laps at the sandbags behind them. The killdeer whistles again. From somewhere far away, the wind blows.

VOLCANO CLIMBER

They said that it was impossible, that the volcano was unpredictable and could erupt without warning. The sky would fill with ash and the fire would spill down the mountainside and sweep me away. But I was born there in the foothills, cradled beneath the ashen sky and the spilling lava, where my father farmed trout and my mother tended the family, and how could I fear the thing that first gave me life?

I was 11, and my sister was sick with a cough that made my mother worry. My brother had moved north to find work. He sent us letters with money, but I would rather have had him. When we were small boys we ran over the foothills of the volcano and we watched the snow falling into the crater at the top. My little sister would tag along behind us. She had always been small, but she was one of us. She was tough. When we fought she could hit as hard as my brother. We dared each other to climb the highest boulders we could find. I wasn't very good at climbing, so my sister would climb first and help pull me up while my brother lifted me from below. And then the three of us would stand high up in the air and yell until the echoes carried our voices far down to the valley below the volcano.

I played on the foothills often after my brother was gone, but I was not yet strong enough to climb far, although I wanted to. I once climbed in the monsoon season. The rain and clouds covered the top of the mountain and I wanted to know what it felt like to be hidden in the storm. When my father found me soaked and curled up underneath a tree just beyond his farm he was angry. He told me it was high time I got some sense, now that my brother was gone and I was the oldest son. But I did not see any sense down there in the foothills. Down where my sister had grown sick with a cough that kept our whole family awake all night, and we could not afford to send her to the doctor. Where my brother had to leave school to travel north and find work. Where my father spent all day farming in the mountains and still my stomach growled. I wondered if sense might be high up among the clouds that circled the volcano.

And then came the day that my sister's coughing expanded to fill the house like smoke. "We must take her to the doctor," my mother said, and my father counted the money from my brother and shook his head. "We can eat a little less and wear our clothes a little longer," said my mother. They found a neighbor with a truck, and he drove them down to the city below the foothills, with my mother holding my sister in the cab while my father bounced up and down in the back. But the next night they had returned, and they dropped their heads in sorrow and said that the doctor could not help my sister anymore, that she was too far gone.

And that was the night that I stood in the foothills and I yelled to the gods or to the stars or the moon or whatever was up there. I yelled for my sister with her sweaty cough and for my brother far away from his family and for my aching stomach that curled inside me in hunger and rage. And in response, the earth shook and the volcano growled and the smoke filled the night and blackened the moon. And I began to climb.

I hardly knew I was doing it, but there I was, already past my father's trout farm, traveling upward into the forests that I had never seen before. My anger carried me, and I felt it resonate deep in the rumbles of the mountain below my feet. All night I hiked, across streams and over fallen logs and through overgrown brush, until the trail finally disappeared and the faintest hint of gold shone from behind the mountain. Birds flew across the sunrise, nothing more than black silhouettes against the light. Above me the smoke curled into the sky and I considered turning back, back to the safety of my village where my father would scold me and my mother would wrap me in a warm blanket she had woven herself and feed me spoonfuls of soup and warn me that our family could not handle another sick child. But then perhaps she would lay me on the bed next to my sister, and my sister's coughing would shake the room, and my parents' sorrow would settle in the home like the volcano's ash on a still, cloudless day. Behind me there were no answers.

The sun shone brighter, and the air grew colder and thinner, and I climbed higher. I could see the crevices near the volcano's top by then, and beneath my feet the mountain growled. I reminded myself that it had not truly erupted in years, nothing more than smoke and ash, at least, and maybe a few flames, but I knew that even the most experienced hikers would not climb this far. The smoke seemed near enough to touch now. I stretched out my hand to feel it. And then I began to cough, a cough that started small and weak and then grew deeper and stronger until it scraped against the edges of my lungs and I felt them turning red. I remembered my sister and night after night of listening to her cough beside me in bed. "I am climbing for you," I whispered into the wind. And then I said it louder. "For her! I am climbing for her!" And then I turned and faced the world below the mountains and I yelled as loud as I could. "Do you hear that, world? I am climbing for my sister. If you want to kill someone, come and kill me." The wind caught my words and I watched it carry them down the mountain to the cities and villages below.

I began running then, and the mountain came to my aid. When my foot landed too heavily, the mountain shook and threw me back into the air. The clouds swirled around me and lifted me up. The crater whistled and cheered and called to me to climb higher and faster. The mountain wanted my sister to live as much as I did, for

she had been born on its foothills too. I ran faster and faster, my feet
lit by the volcano's burning embers. Then I was at the top. I bent
over and caught my breath from the climb and then crept to the
edge of the crater. Inside it burned deep orange and blue, and I saw it
working, fighting against the earth, against the pain and the sickness
and disease, cleaning it all with fire. I felt its anger, even stronger than
mine, and I knew it had been waiting for me to come to it, so that it
could show me how it too hated how hard my father worked and how
loudly my sister coughed. I stood tall and threw my hands in the air.
The world spun out around me, red light fading to purple fading to
morning dimness, where people still slept in their homes unaware of
the volcano's fury against their pain.

I stood at the top and looked at the fire raging, and I knew that
my sister was better. My climbing had healed her. The volcano had
healed her. My whole life it had smoked and seethed and waited for
me to climb to it so that it could do what it had always longed to do.
I ran down the mountain. The sun rose, and the sweat dripped down
my face but I hardly noticed. I ran through the foothills and straight
to my house and through the door and into my parents' room where
my sister lay calm and sleeping and healthy. My parents stood next
to her and watched her sleep. "Her coughing stopped this morning,"
they said. "It's a miracle." I told them it was not a miracle. I told them
how I had climbed and what I had seen. How on the volcano's edge
I had seen anger I never knew existed, that it was waiting and ready
to help me. They took my sister back to the doctors in the city to see
what they would say, but the doctors scratched their heads and said
they couldn't account for the miraculous healing.

My sister grew stronger every day. She began to walk again, and
then run, and soon we were climbing on the foothills and wading in
the streams at our father's farm. She would leap up the foothills and
I would chase her, and when we fought I knew to duck because she
could hit as hard as a boy again. Some mornings we would sit in the
foothills and she would ask me to tell her about the climb and so I

would, and her favorite part was always when I got to the top and saw how much the volcano cared about her.

We were happy then, but my father said it was not fair to keep the volcano a secret. He said the rest of the world deserved to know what had happened. We owed it to them.

At first no one believed me, and so I had to show them. I found another volcano, a small one this time, but violent. I asked the helicopters to follow me to watch me climb, and, just like before, when I neared the top, the volcano reached down and pulled me up so that I could see the anger that burned in the crater. This time it was a woman in a coma who was healed. She woke up to her children around her bed, and the doctors who had said it was time to let her life end did not have any answers. Then the interviews piled up, one show after another. They offered me magazine features and plastered my photo in the windows of sporting good stores. They asked me what I wanted, how they could pay me, and I said I wanted nothing but for my family to be together, my sister healthy, my brother living with us again. So they flew my brother back to us and arranged for him to go to school and the three of us climbed and played and laughed.

Now the world cheers me on. "The Boy Who Climbs Volcanoes," they call me. For three years I have been climbing volcanoes for them. They send me from mountain to mountain so that I can climb to the top and peer into the crater and tell them what I see. Sponsors give me flame-proof clothing with their logos embroidered in bold across my chest. Nutrition companies name energy drinks after me. My father once asked if this was really how I wanted to spend my teenage years, and I said how could I not? Experienced climbers have tried to do what I do, but they cannot reach the top. They were not born beneath the volcano's shadow like I was. The world needs me. All over the world I hike volcanoes, active or inactive, the frequently climbed or the desolate. And every single time, when I near the top, the mountain rushes down to pull me up, the way my sister and brother helped me climb the boulder years ago. Each time, I relearn how much the volcanoes want to be climbed, want to help us.

Talk show hosts interview me. "Where did you find your inspiration, your courage?" they ask me. They say that my climbs give the world hope, something to cheer for. "We need someone on our side," they say. "That's you."

In return, I tell them how the world does not know anger until it sees the anger inside a volcano's crater. I tell them that the mountains rage for us, at the injustice and hurt we experience. I tell them of this mighty ally, and they clap for me and the people ask me to climb another for them.

They fly me to a desert, and I climb a volcano that smokes into the bluest sky. The sand and wind rub against my skin. I tie a bandana around my mouth so that I will not cough. At the top this volcano's fire burns deep red, darker than the other volcanoes, and when the helicopters lift me from the crater and bring me back down, all of the villages nearby have clean water and the children can drink their fill without becoming sick. I climb one in the rainforest. It hisses and seethes, a young and passionate anger. After I climb, the trees that have been torn down by machines grow tall and strong again and fill with monkeys and parrots. Near a large city a volcano's rage is deep quiet, a rumble that shakes the earth in silence. I climb, and fathers stop beating their children.

My family lives in comfort now. We own a large house in the city below my volcano. We will never lack for anything again. Medical bills and college tuition and my parents' retirement—the volcanoes have kept us safe and provided for us. My father does not need to work on the foothills until dark, and my brother lives with us and goes to school again, and my sister is strong enough to run. They call me hero, the savior of the family.

In three years I have climbed some of the most dangerous volcanoes on the planet, but they ask me to climb one more, larger than any mountain I have ever seen, roaring and unclimbable. "If you can climb this one, you can climb anything," they say. They will be right with me they whole time, with backup and rescue if I need it. Think of what climbing this one could accomplish. The preparations take weeks. Tactical teams discuss possible routes with me. Sponsors outfit me with the best gear. Fans send letters and emails and say that they believe in me, that they know I can climb this final, most difficult volcano. The world fills with hope. On the morning of the climb crowds surround me and cheer. They write their wishes on banners and wave them high: "No more poverty!" "Find the cure to cancer!" "End global warming!" My father puts his hand on my shoulder and says to focus on him. He says that whatever happens, he is proud of me. He reminds me that nothing is as important as my safety and says to be careful. My brother tousles my hair like he did when we were children and says, "Let me know if you need a lift." My sister holds my hand. "Thank you," she says, and I hug her tight.

I start out slow. I take my time on the foothills and save my strength for the top. But from the beginning, this climb feels different. The forests are quiet, and the trees still. I hear the helicopter hovering above my head and the crowds cheering behind me, but nothing else. Soon the path grows steeper, the sun hotter. I take frequent breaks. I am not used to feeling this tired. I remember the climbing techniques my trainers taught me, how to lock my knees to save oxygen. I focus my breathing and climb. The crowds fade and soon I am alone. I feel my feet against the mountain. It is unaware of me. Higher up, I feel the first rumbles of anger that I've come to expect. They are low and faint at first. They tremor beneath my feet and fill my body with fear. The air is heavy, calm.

Then, a roar. The mountain explodes, the earth cracks. This anger is violent, uncontrolled, blind. It tosses me from one side of the path to the other. I cling to a tree and crouch low for protection and try to crawl forward. I wait for the mountain to recognize me, so that it can pick me up like it always does and carry me to the top. But this one doesn't notice me, and even if it did, I know it wouldn't matter. Its anger is too strong, and it does not care that I climb it to make the world a better place. I feel it raging hot white beneath my feet, and I almost turn back. But I know I can do it. I know I can climb to the top and the mountain will see me at last and the world will be healed. I stop for the night to set up camp.

My sleeping bag is warm and thick, and I build a fire. I touch my hands to the mountain and whisper to it. "Please let me up," I say. "Do not let me fail." It shakes, gently this time, and I fall asleep and know that tomorrow the mountain will be on my side.

In the night, though, the volcano's rage spills over, flaming and boiling and hot, and it consumes the earth. I watch it burn the forests and grass, and then I run. I run as fast as I can, and when the lava has almost overpowered me I grab the branch of a tree and scale to the top. The helicopter signals to me through the smoke and lifts me up, above the seething volcano that does not want to be climbed. When I am inside, they clear my lungs of smoke and they pat my arm and say, "It is all right. You tried your best." I try to fight them, to explain what happened and to watch the mountain burn, but the smoke makes my head foggy and I am asleep.

When I am well I return to my family. My parents say they are just glad I am all right, that they are proud of me for trying. But the next day, my sister begins to cough again. It is not strong, but I recognize the sound in an instant. My parents run to her, and my mother phones the doctor. They take my sister to the hospital right away. This time, she does not get better. The doctors prescribe the strongest treatments, but nothing works.

"Whatever she needs, we can pay for it," I say, but they say that is not the issue anymore. They say it must have been in remission, the disease just lurking in her body all these years, held off by something no one could explain. Their eyes hold pity, they tried their best. Outside of the hospital the world wants to know what it was like on the mountain that I could not climb, with the lava raining down and the earth quaking. They are perhaps more excited by my failure than they would have been by my success. "Not now," I tell the reporters. "Leave me be."

I watch my sister slip away. She moans in pain and she is so weak that she cannot talk to me. I sit in a chair next to her bed and hold her hand. Her fingertips squeeze mine, and I whisper to her that I am sorry. I don't understand why I failed. My brother suggests I climb our volcano again, but I know that wouldn't help this time. I don't leave the hospital. My mother's eyes are dark and tired. She looks older than she ever looked in our concrete home in the foothills. I watch the pain etch itself into the wrinkles on her face. It attaches itself to her bones and she slumps against its weight. My father stands next to her and holds her hand. He raises her fingers to his lips and kisses them. My brother moves to my sister's bed and tries to make her laugh. He reminds her of our childhood on the volcano, and she smiles for a moment but it takes too much strength so she falls asleep.

I stand near the doorway and watch them all, and I feel sorrow turning to rage inside me, boiling, ready to erupt, blind and hot like the last volcano. I turn and run, down the hallway and into the waiting room where a young couple cries over their miscarried child. Their eyes narrow at me like they know my climb should have stopped this, but they were not on the mountain with me, alone with its impossible fury. I kick at chairs and pound my fist into the wall and they hurry away. My father finds me there. Despite my years of climbing he is still larger than me, and he holds my arms still until I am calm.

"This is not your fault," he says to me. "You did what you could, but you cannot save her, no matter how many volcanoes you climb."

I run from him, I run outside and face the nearest volcano, and I yell, like I did the night my sister almost died, the night I first climbed. I yell for the injustice of it all, and I yell because despite the miles and miles that my feet have traveled, it is not far enough and never will be, and I yell for the ways we can save each other and the ways we cannot, the volcanoes we can climb and the ones that boil over. I yell for my sister and the person she will not become. Smoke curls into the sky and turns the world gray. I know I will not climb again. From inside the hospital my mother begins her long and endless wail.

GOODNESS AND MERCY

There was this bird. A baby sparrow or something, still partially unhatched. It had fallen from its nest and the ants were starting to notice. My sister and I found it while playing in the backyard. Its skin was translucent, almost blue, and its eyes were still shut, but it was struggling to be free from its speckled shell, straining wings like sticky paper mache. We broke the shell up piece by piece and got the bird out, and we wrapped it in an old t-shirt to keep it warm and fed it bites of birdseed that we ground to a powder. The bird couldn't see us, but we whistled to it, and it peeped back, its beak gaping open and shut. We named it Mordecai, and that night we woke up every hour to check on it. We could see it getting stronger. It started to lift its head when we whistled to it, like it knew who we were. In the morning, though, it began to fade. We sang to it and asked it to live, just for us, because we already loved it, but it died in our hands. We buried it in a little shoebox under the pecan tree in the back yard. We put a pile of rocks on its grave to remember, and we didn't know what to pray so we recited the Twenty-Third Psalm. "The Lord is my shepherd; I shall not want," we said. My sister was younger than me. She held my hand and cried while we prayed. "He makes me lie down in green pastures. He restores my soul…Surely goodness and mercy shall follow me all the days of my life, and I will dwell in the house of the Lord forever." When we finished our prayer we threw flowers on the grave, like we'd seen people do in movies, and then we sang the doxology.

When I was a girl my dad beat my mom. Nothing bad, just a shove here or there, a slap, a punch, a black eye or a busted lip. Nothing makeup couldn't hide. Nothing to call the cops over, although I used to lie awake and listen.

I wanted him to stop, but I was just a kid, and he was my dad. "Daddy's girl," he called me, and I knew I was his favorite. I was the one he reached for when he came home from work, lifted me high above his shoulders while I gripped his black curls and held on tight, wrapped me up in a blanket, long arms and legs flailing, and swung me around and around the living room, me laughing, peering through holes, the room through the spinning blanket a river of colors encircling me. I was the one he taught to fish, and to shoot, and to shift the gears on his truck while he drove, and when he told me I looked tough in my sneakers and baseball cap it was the best compliment I knew.

My friend Isaac changed things. I was twelve then, and we weren't great friends, but we were both kind of loners and would sit on the swings at recess and read comics together. I knew things were bad at his home, but I never knew how bad till the day he and his sister hid in a corner while their dad beat their mom to death with a shovel. It doesn't sound real. Before then I didn't think stuff like that happened in this world, but now I know it does all the time. Afterward Isaac and his sister looked changed, like they'd learned something that other kids hadn't yet. I wanted to talk about it. I wanted to ask Isaac how it felt to sit there and watch something so awful happening, like did he feel helpless, or scared, or maybe had he been just numb, like he was watching a movie and not his own real life? I wanted to know if it was like when I listened to my parents in their bedroom next to mine, my father's voice, first low and discontent, maybe only a whisper, then growing to a roar, the sharp crack of his belt against the air, the rattle of the floor shaking beneath his heavy feet, and then my mother's whimpers. I wanted to ask if there had been any clues. But of course Isaac didn't want to talk about it, just wanted to pretend that nothing had happened and get back to reading comics on the swings.

One morning I came down to breakfast, and my mom hadn't put on her makeup yet. I'd heard her the night before. She always tried to keep quiet, but my bedroom was next to theirs, and I heard her every time, crying, begging my dad to please stop, like my sister and I begged him when he tickled us too hard, the way he sometimes did, when he held us down and dug bruises into our ribs and we laughed and laughed at first but then were crying and screaming for him to let us go, in the grip of something we didn't quite understand but knew to fear. I didn't know how to predict when he was going to hurt my mom or how it started. Just that something flipped inside him and he became a different person. My sister always came into my bed and curled up next to me. "They'll be okay," I told her, because I was the oldest and it was my job to say that.

I slid onto the barstool at the kitchen counter, where my sister and I ate breakfast every morning. She was fixing our favorite, scrambled eggs and French toast, which was how I knew it had been a bad night. It was her way of making the world good again, I guess, her own small way of fighting against the darkness, and I guess we all do that. My dad was already at work, and she was fixing three plates. She was sniffling, her eyes still swollen from crying, a welt rising on her cheek. She looked small, weak, a child, and I wanted to be someone other than her daughter, her father or her mother or even her husband, someone who could protect her from the things that were hurting her.

"He's gotta stop, Mom," I said. "If he doesn't, I'm calling the cops."

"Sweetie," she said, and she passed me my plate and a fork. "I know this is so hard for you to understand, but it's better this way." She told me things could be so much worse. "Remember that boy at your school?" She said that if it got reported my sister and I could end up in foster care. Really bad things could happen. "The system is so broken," she said. And she asked me if I wanted that for my sister.

I knew then that it was up to me. There was no one else who would protect her. I wasn't going to crouch in a corner and watch it all happen, no matter how much I loved my dad. I would save my mom. I would save my whole family, and not just my family, but Isaac too. I would show him that things could get better, that he didn't need to feel so powerless.

That week I couldn't eat. My dad asked what was wrong with me, and I told him it was nothing. He rumpled my hair and said, "Don't you lie to me. I know you better than that. You're my girl." I think he really did know something was going on because he was on really good behavior and for a while things were okay.

It happened a couple weeks later. My dad was so happy that night. At the dinner table he kept teasing my sister. He'd tell her to look at something out the window, a dinosaur or an elephant or something ridiculous like that, and she'd play along, and when her head was turned, he'd scoop another spoonful of green beans onto her plate. He did it again and again, till her plate was nothing but a mountain of green beans and we were all laughing. After dinner I usually washed the dishes, but that night he said he'd take over for me, so I could finish the game of Scrabble my sister and I had started. He pretended he wanted to do it. "It'll keep my hands warm," he said. "It sure is a cold night." Before bed he read to us. We were in the middle of *Oliver Twist*, and we'd just gotten to the good part where Oliver gets taken in by Rose and there's a little break from all the sadness.

I was leaning on his shoulder while he read, following along in the book, and when he read a word wrong I'd correct him and he'd swat at me as if he were annoyed. My sister was sitting next to my mom, and I thought while he was reading how happy we all were, how picture perfect.

I woke up in the middle of the night to the sound of my dad shouting and throwing things, and then I heard my mom scream the way she usually did, muffled, like she didn't want us to hear. I tried to go back to sleep. I tried to pretend it was something else, maybe just a neighbor or an angry cat. Then there was another crash, louder this time, and another scream. I was ready. I knew what to do. I wasn't the type to back down once I'd made up my mind. There was a phone in the hallway, and I'd practiced dialing again and again. Punching three numbers sounds simple enough, but it's not. When you're making the call that you know will break up your family, betray the person you love most, three numbers is the hardest thing in the world, even if you know it's right.

It didn't take long after I reported it. We heard the sirens coming down the block, and when they stopped in front of our house the whole family gathered downstairs. "What have you done?" my mom said to me. There was blood dripping from one of her ears, and her cheek was bruised. Not enough time to hide it.

The next hour was a haze of officers and questions and explanations. I remember they asked my dad to come with them quietly. If things got too violent, they'd have to take us girls away too and put us in foster care. Things could get complicated. It was for our own protection.

"I'll go," said my dad. "I don't want their lives disrupted." They let him get a few things, and I heard him thumping around upstairs in his bedroom and I almost ran up to the officers and said it had just been a practical joke, that I was just mad about something or other and trying to pay him back. Before my dad left he looked at me, and I looked down at my feet. "I love you, baby girl," he whispered, right then his best and most gentle self, and he kissed me on the top of my head.

In the following weeks there were visits from caseworkers and court dates and meetings with therapists. My mom cried a lot, more than she had before my dad left, and every time I saw my dad he looked small and I wanted to wrap my arms around him and comfort him. It's funny, in those weeks after my dad left all I could think about was that bird named Mordecai. Its clear cold skin and the helpless way its tiny beak gasped for air as it died.

I didn't understand when I was a kid the extent of my own inability to end the suffering in this world. I still don't understand it really.

I grew up and became a social worker. It was the only thing I could become. There was never any choice. I specialized in abuse prevention, but the prevention often came too late. I saw the worst things, things you wouldn't believe yet still have to. Things that are too absurd and too horrible to be fiction. Sometimes I saved lives. I went home at night knowing that a child would live at least a little bit longer because of a decision I'd made. Other times I made the wrong call, and children who were in my care were hurt, even killed. That was the nature of being a social worker. I could have done something easier with my life, but what? I think I was born to fight. Besides, terrible things were going to happen to these kids with or without me—that was what Isaac had taught me, what my dad taught me—but at least this way I could stop it every now and then.

My mother and I didn't talk much once I left for college. I saw her sometimes. She and my dad divorced, and she remarried when I was in graduate school. Her husband wore suits and worked in an office, but my sister was a doctor, her own way of fighting, and every so often she told me that my mom had been to the ER with a broken clavicle, a dislocated shoulder, bruising on her ribs that she needed pain meds for. In the end, whatever was going to happen was going to happen.

My father and I were close, though. He was there at my graduation, and the day I moved into my first apartment. I'd forgiven him, or he'd forgiven me, depending on which side of the story you're on. I still didn't know if I'd done the right thing, if I'd actually saved anybody that night or only made things harder. He and I didn't talk about it, although sometimes I thought I felt his distrust when he looked at me.

I was at work late this past Friday night, starting the paperwork for a new case, a particularly confusing one. We'd gotten a call about a baby covered in third-degree burns, the father, the baby's primary caregiver, a fifteen-year-old boy who claimed it was an accident. We were investigating, trying to figure out who was to blame, who was the victim who needed protecting. It was one of those cases with no clear villain, which is more common than you'd think. I would visit the hospital in the morning to determine if the baby should be removed or if the boy only needed parenting lessons, needed to learn that when your child is cold, you cannot warm her with a blow drier against her skin, that you have to be wiser than a teenager, even if that is all you are. I was almost finished for the night when my coworker came in with the local newspaper. She pointed to a headline: "Argyle High Alumni Dies in Five-Car Pile-Up."

"Did you see this?" she asked. "Isn't that the same high school you attended?"

Above the headline was a picture of Isaac with his arm around his sister. I hadn't talked to him in years, not since we'd graduated from high school, and even before that it wasn't often. We'd never become close after what happened, but I thought about him. He was the boy whose story I used to shape my own life, and I guess I feel bad about that, that in the end that's all he was to me. The story I pulled out in college when I sat in class and had to say why I wanted to be a social worker. Why I wanted to save the world. "There was this boy I knew."

"Yeah," I said. "I went to school with him."

"Article says he had a sister but no other family. They look close." She handed the paper to me. "Sorry for your loss," she said.

Outside the night was clear and cold. The cloud cover from the day had dispersed, and under the stars the temperature had dropped. It was still early in winter. The weather was hard to predict. I'd left my coat at home, so I wrapped my arms around my chest and shivered. Something scurried at the side of the road, a possum or maybe a raccoon. I stopped at this little restaurant I liked and got takeout. Chinese food.

It felt wrong every time, how life went on after tragedy. How a baby could be injured, and I would still eat Szechuan chicken. A young man with a terrible childhood could die too young, but I still shivered and wished for a coat in the cold.

I lived in a small apartment near my office. I was still paying off graduate school loans. The apartment wasn't much, but I didn't need much. I was content enough there. I had a couch and a bed and a kitchen table, a few photos I'd hung of a trip my sister and I had taken around Europe. Simple, but good. I sat down that night with my dinner and poured a glass of wine. I turned on my heater, and a puff of dust blew out of the vents. I guess I hadn't used it yet that season. Isaac was dead, I told myself, and thought about it. I should have felt surprised, but I didn't. I stacked up all the stories I'd seen in the past months, and I thought about all the darkness in this world, how it keeps coming and coming and never stops.

I scrolled through my phone and found Isaac's sister's number from high school. I almost tried calling it, just so I could feel like I was doing something, but even if the number hadn't changed, what would I say? "I'm sorry for your loss"? "How could this have happened"? "He didn't deserve this"?

I was about halfway finished with dinner when someone knocked on the door. It was too late for visitors, but my downstairs neighbors were night owls and sometimes asked to borrow things at strange hours when they hadn't gone to the grocery store. I peered through the peephole just in case but figured it would be them.

Instead it was a woman. About my size, maybe a little bit shorter. She wore a big puffy jacket, and a ski cap over dull tangled red hair, and most of her teeth were missing but her smile was bright.

"Hello, ma'am," she said when I'd opened the door. "My name's Suzy. I'm sorry it's so late, but I'm wondering if you've got a few minutes." I looked back at my dinner, but I didn't really have a good excuse to hurry away, so I said sure.

She was a magazine saleswoman, and that night she was going door-to-door trying to get people to subscribe. She didn't look like she'd had much success, and I felt sorry for her. Her life was easy enough to read from the missing teeth and dirty clothes and matted hair. I didn't need any magazines, but I said I would subscribe to a couple anyway. It was a small mercy, the universe sending me a tangible way I could help someone on a night I felt so overwhelmed with helplessness.

"Do you have one about cooking?" I said. "Something simple, because I don't have lots of time."

"Sure," said Suzy, and she pointed me to a few that would work. I chose one for cooking and one for running, not that I was much of a runner. We were both getting chilly standing there in the doorway, so I asked her in out of the cold while I was filling out the subscription. She stood there looking too big for my house, afraid to move in case she touched anything. With the door closed, I smelled her, even though I wasn't trying to, everything from her thick unwashed coat to the cigarettes on her breath. I sat down and started writing.

"Would you like anything?" I asked her. "Some water or something?"

She said she'd like that. I didn't have any bottled water, so I asked her if a glass was all right, and she said sure, and I invited her to sit down. I saw her looking over my table, my half-eaten dinner and the bottle of wine.

Her eyes went hungry and wanting. I'd seen that look before, so many times. I'd seen it on the parents who let their kids raise themselves so that they can get the next fix, or the ones screaming in withdrawal. I saw that look in her eyes, and I felt a little thrill.

This was the mercy I so needed, that on a night when I felt so helpless to save anyone, my mother, or Isaac, or the children in my care, here was something I could do, a clear and unblurred line, a right versus a wrong.

I started to think through which people I could call, which places that could take her in and help her detox. If she had children we'd have to find them a safe place to live. Or maybe they had a place already, since it was late and their mother was out selling magazines.

I picked up my phone, the list of numbers ready in my head, and then I saw Isaac's picture and the newspaper headline that announced his premature death, and I thought of my mother, and I remembered:

In the end, whatever was going to happen was going to happen, with or without me.

I set the phone down. "Sorry about that," I said. "I'm just finishing dinner. Could I maybe offer you a glass of wine?"

That was what I wanted to see. That look that swept over her face. Total and complete joy, relief.

"You sure?" she said.

"Of course. I insist." I pulled a glass off the shelf and filled it with wine and handed it to her. She drank it like it was a shot of whiskey and then stood up.

"Thank you," she said. "That was nice. I should be going now."

"Not yet, I still need to fill out this subscription. Sit down and have a bit more," I said. "It's cold out." So she sat again, and I poured her another glass, we got to talking.

"You live around here?" I asked her.

"Not too near," she told me. "A bus ride away." I sipped my wine and printed my address on the form, and she told me about her life. It wasn't more tragic than most, but still plenty hard. A few bad breaks—sick kids, a fire, debt.

"Since the fire it's just been a struggle to make it, you know?" she said.

"Yeah," I said. "I get it."

"Like we're almost there and something comes and pushes us down again," said Suzy. "Like there was this one time, my first son, Joseph, he wanted to go to Chuck E. Cheese's for his birthday, and he was so excited, I wish you could have seen him, just jumping up and down and up and down, inviting all his friends. We were just starting to have money again, and we hadn't done anything fun like that for the kids in a while. Then two days before the party, the little one comes down with a case of pneumonia. It turns real bad, and he has to go to the hospital and get hooked up to a respirator and get on medicine, and those hospital bills, they aren't cheap. Joseph, though, he was a real good sport. I was real proud of him."

"That's rough," I said, then nodded toward the magazines and asked, "You make much doing that?"

"A bit," she said. "Enough to keep food in my kids' bellies. They're with their grandmother tonight. She watches them when I'm working. Their daddy's long gone."

"Yeah," I said. "I've seen that before." She shouldn't be here tonight, drinking glasses of wine and not making much money. She should be selling more magazine subscriptions, or home with her children getting sober, and I should be preparing for the next investigation, figuring out the next person I have to protect. Meeting another way, she and I would be enemies, and I knew I should tell her to go, but I was so tired of this fight.

"My food will go cold just sitting here," I said. "You want some of it?" She said sure, and I pulled out another plate to split my chicken fried rice. "How about a bit more wine to go with that meal?" I asked. I split the last of the bottle between our two glasses and slid hers over to her.

She swallowed her wine and asked, "What about you? Family?"

I pointed to the photos on the fridge. "Father, mother, sister," I said. "Don't see my mom much these days, but the rest of us are close."

"That's nice," she said. "Family is nice."

"Yeah, they can be," I said.

"I had a sister once," she said. "She's dead now."

"I'm sorry to hear that," I said. "That must be hard to live with."

"It is what it is," she said. She unzipped her coat and slipped her arms from the sleeves. "Mind if I take this off?" she asked. "I'm getting kind of warm."

"Of course not. Make yourself at home."

The heat was starting to kick in by then, and my apartment smelled like burning dust. I liked it, the smell of winter arriving at last. I heard my downstairs neighbor yelling at her teenage daughter. They lived there alone, the two of them, and they fought a lot. I didn't know what to do about it, except loan them eggs or milk when they asked for it. I turned the thermostat down and offered Suzy a glass of water.

"What do you do?" Suzy asked me. "You sell magazines too?" She winked. I laughed and told her no, I was a social worker.

"Guess you've seen lots of sad stuff," she said.

"Yeah, but good stuff too. Sometimes."

"That's why you come home and drink wine," she said.

"I saved this kid's life yesterday," I told her. "At least I think I did. For now."

"That's good. Must make you feel like a hero."

"Not really. I know I'm not."

I hoped she would contradict me, tell me all my work wasn't for nothing, everything I'd ever done to save people starting back when I was twelve, although I hadn't told her—or anyone else, really—about that.

"Tell me some of what you've seen," she said instead. "It'll make me feel like I'm not such a bad mother."

I told her story after story, names left out of course, and details changed. I told her about the father who fed his five-year-old only jars of baby food to keep her tired, and the mother who locked her children in the bathroom and set the house on fire, and the boy and his new baby tonight. I wasn't trying to shock her. I was only telling her the world I knew. It's how I saw it. I looked at people and saw all the ways they could hurt each other and be hurt.

I could feel the wine hitting my blood by then, warming me and filling me with something that felt like safety. Suzy was looking at me with pity, as if I were the one who needed help, not her, and I wanted to tell her everything. "There was this bird," I wanted to say. And, "When I was a girl my dad beat my mom," I wanted to say. I wanted to tell her every single sad thing I'd seen my whole life, one stacked up after the other, so that she could feel their weight the way I always did.

"It's hard. You know? You want to save them all."

We were quiet, both unsure if or how to lighten the conversation. I glanced up to the wine rack by kitchen counter, where I had a couple other bottles of wine. Nothing fancy or expensive, just a few basic varieties on hand for when I needed them and didn't want to go to the store. "Want to split another one?" I asked.

"Gladly," she said. I picked out a red from the rack, something rich and fruity, and pulled out the cork, and she nodded her approval.

"It's right there in the Bible," she said. "The Twenty-Third Psalm. My cup runneth over. God knew we needed this stuff."

"Surely goodness and mercy shall follow me," I said, and poured the wine.

I don't know how long we talked. Hours and hours probably, all night long. We finished that bottle and started on another. Downstairs the neighbors had stopped yelling. They must have gone to bed. The wind was blowing harder and louder, and the windowpane was starting to steam from the heat inside and the growing cold out. I brought out some crackers so we'd have something to nibble on. We talked about her sister, who was sick, and about my sister, and about Suzy's two little boys and all the funny things they said. She asked me if I was going to have kids, and I said probably not, after everything I'd seen, but who knows. She said she got that, but don't give up on the idea yet, that she didn't know what her life would be without her kids. She knew she needed to change, get her drinking under control, find a better job, but things could be much worse, and that had everything to do with her boys.

"They keep me in this world," she said. "Maybe I'll bring them over to meet you some day. So you can see how funny they are."

"I'd like that," I said.

"The older one does this thing. He pulls his pants around his knees so his legs are tied together, and he waddles around like a penguin. Then his little brother just cracks up." She stood up and started to demonstrate. She wrapped her purse strap around her knees and waddled around and held her hands at her side, like Dick Van Dyke in *Mary Poppins*. She was drunk by then—we both were—and she lost her balance, and came crashing to the ground. She pulled the tablecloth down with her, and both of our wine glasses and the half-full bottle, the wine dripping off her nose and ears like she was standing in the rain without an umbrella, and her just sitting there in the middle of the floor surrounded by broken glass and the stained tablecloth and laughing.

"Is that how he does it?" I said. "Just like that with the wine and everything?" I reached out a hand to help her up, and she pulled me down too.

"Just like that," she said. She stuck out her tongue to lick a drop of wine from the tip of her nose. "Just picture how funny it'd be with a five-year-old."

We were both laughing by then, can't-breathe, tears-streaming, doubled-over laughter. I hadn't laughed that hard in a long time, maybe ever.

Suzy fell asleep on my couch. The next morning when I woke up she would be gone. She wouldn't leave a number or address, or any sign that she'd been here at all except the empty wine bottles and the pillows on the couch a little bit wrinkled and the broken glasses on the floor. I would look for a note or something but wouldn't find one.

At Isaac's funeral, his sister wouldn't be able to stop crying. They'd been close, the way siblings become close when they are all alone against the world. I would hug her, and she would say, "What a pointless death." Do you ever have those moments where it feels like everything your whole life is coming together to a point, like it's all related somehow, and it's telling you exactly who you are? That morning at the funeral I would think of it all, the dead bird, and Isaac, and calling the cops on my father, and becoming a social worker, and this strange night with the alcoholic saleswoman, how our sorrow and our laughter had come so near each other, and in it all I would see the shape of my life, what it had been and what it would continue to be. I wouldn't mind it then, the long and maybe pointless fight. It would be a beautiful morning, the kind that only comes along a few times a year. Clouds like mountains, paintbrushes beginning to bloom across the fields, birds chasing each other through the trees. We would recite the Twenty-Third Psalm. Then we would drop flowers on the grave, and the minister would say a prayer, and the birds would dig up worms for their young, and someone in the crowd would sing out one note to start us off, clear and strong, and we'd sing the doxology.

TORNADO SEASON

My little brother was fifteen when I talked to him for the first time in over a decade. He found me online and messaged me his number. "Call me sis," he wrote. "Now." It was noon on a Wednesday, but he said was playing hooky from school, smoking cigarettes in his garage while his grandmother napped, so I called.

I was twenty-nine then, finishing up my doctorate in English literature, making a living teaching freshman composition and helping high schoolers practice SAT vocabulary. That spring I was busy studying for my comprehensive exams. They were only three weeks away, and after that all I'd have left was my dissertation, no small task, true, but small compared to the years of graduate work I'd already put into this degree.

Tornado season that spring was unpredictable and abusive. The storms hit without warning, tearing through towns, destroying property, uprooting trees, terrifying animals, leaving behind broken fences and hot sunshine. I'd grown up in Tornado Alley and was used to one or two towns being destroyed every spring, but there was something strange happening that year, some perfect and terrible combination of high and low pressure that threatened to wipe out the entire region.

The day Josh and I reconnected was one of those sparkling post-thunderstorm days, the kind that seems to be mocking you for being so afraid, the grass tall and bright, the birds loud, the sky clear.

"Guess what color my hair is, sis," he said.

"Brown. I've seen your picture on Facebook, remember?"

"Nah, black. I dyed it," he said. "Black hair, black shirt, black jeans, black boots, black studded belt. Then don't nobody mess with me."

Josh bragged to me about how he'd been in jail six times already, had ten girlfriends in the past year, would spend his whole life stoned and drunk if he weren't on parole. He could bring a man to the ground five different ways if he had to, he said. He was athletic but not much into sports, preferred things with more violence.

I remembered the long blond curls that hung in his eyes. The way at night his eyelashes brushed his cheek as soft as crepe myrtle blossoms in June. The heavy feel of his head resting on my chest while he woke up each morning. His wet arms wrapped around my neck after a bath.

We weren't brother and sister exactly, not in the way other kids are brothers and sisters. He was my half brother, my dad's son, the dad I never saw much, since my mom kicked him out before I was even born. Josh had lived with my mom and me when he was a baby so he didn't have to go into foster care, his own mother only a teenager. But my mom had always said it couldn't be permanent. She had enough worry as a single mother without taking on extra children who weren't even hers. It was just to keep him out of foster care until a long-term home came along. Before he was two he'd been adopted by his grandmother, his mom's mom, and after a couple years we lost touch entirely.

"You like Johnny Cash?" he asked.

"Who doesn't?"

"Then listen to this, sis," he said, and he started to sing. He sang through a bunch of songs: "Sunday Morning Coming Down," and "Help Me Make It Through The Night," and "Walk The Line," and he had a good voice for the genre, the right amount of twang masking the right amount of troubled past. I could hear a guitar in the background and guessed he was probably strumming along while he sang.

"That was wonderful, little brother," I said when he finished. "It feels so good to hear your voice again."

"I bet it does," he said.

I'd grown up in Dallas. It was just my mom and me until Josh came along, and then just the two of us again after he left. I was her everything, the way Josh was mine for a few years. Every single thing she did was for me—every late night she worked, and meal she skipped, and weekend with friends she turned down. I should have loved her more, should have felt more grateful, but she was the reason Josh was gone, and I'd never forgiven her for that.

Once upon a time I'd loved Josh desperately and passionately, as deeply as teenage girls love their boyfriends, or children love their first pets. I was fourteen when he was born, only two years younger than his mother. My own mother was disgusted with my father for getting a teenager pregnant, but I didn't know him well enough to feel anything but curiosity. I saw him at a birthday party every few years, and that was about it, he no more than the tall stranger who had given me his long nose and blond hair. Josh was born with drugs in his system, and he came to live with us almost immediately. My father had called asking if we'd look after him. "It's just till his mom gets out of rehab," he'd said, and I stood in the other room and listened to my mom yell at him until she'd finally agreed. I still don't know if she was doing it for him or for me or for the baby, but it didn't matter to me back then, not after I'd seen him and felt his fingers curl around my own.

Have you ever seen a child going through drug withdrawal? There are things children shouldn't know—how it feels to have their legs broken, what it's like to go without food, to cry endlessly for hours—and drug withdrawal is one of them. Now children are given morphine to help ease the pain, but back then they suffered cold turkey, sweated and cried and shook and trembled until the drugs finally left their eight-pound bodies.

I cried when Josh cried. When his body shook, I felt like my own was shaking too. I didn't know the word "empathy" back in the ninth grade. I'm sure I'd heard it, but I'd never thought about it much, is what I mean, how it's not just a mirroring of emotions but more like an incarnation, a total embodiment of another person's experiences. That's what I felt when I held Josh's convulsing body, like every wave of nausea that hit his system, every loud noise or bright light that scraped against his nerves, every racing beat of his tiny heart, it was all mine.

And then it was over. His body relaxed. He unlearned how to do things a newborn shouldn't know how to do, things—like rolling over and standing up—that had only been possible because of his pain. He learned, gradually, to drink a bottle in under two hours, to sleep without convulsing, and even to smile. It would have all happened with or without me, but I had held him through it all, and I felt at least somewhat responsible for his healing. It was a feeling my ninth-grade classmates, and maybe even my own mother, couldn't know.

"Tell me about this kid," said my boyfriend Robby the night I first called Josh. We were sitting on the couch together, eating a meal he'd cooked for us while the television played endless footage of tornado destruction. Our windows were wide open to the weather. I liked it that way, liked feeling close and connected to whatever was going to happen.

Robby and I had been dating since almost the beginning of graduate school. I'd met him online and immediately loved how different his life was from mine: two parents, a big family with lots of brothers and sisters, a degree in engineering, a well-paying job that let him wear jeans and t-shirts any day of the week. He made me laugh, too, which is something I didn't do well on my own.

"Well I don't know much yet," I said. "Except he wants a lot of attention and doesn't really have anyone looking out for him. His grandmother is old and sick. He's basically raising himself."

"I mean tell me what you remember about him, from before. I've hardly ever heard you talk about him."

A gust of wind knocked a tree branch against the side of the house, and the leaves scattered across our floor. Robby picked them up while I talked to him. I told him a little bit. I told him that Josh had lived with us until he was three, until I was seventeen, that I'd loved him, almost like he was my own son, that he was what I remembered from high school, hurrying home to him each afternoon, ditching my friends, skipping out on volleyball practice or school dances. I'd been an only child before, and that was the first time I felt like someone belonged to me.

"You probably don't know what that's like," I said. Robby was third in his family. He'd always had people.

"Josh loved me as much as I loved him," I said. "I was his first mother."

"It must have been hard when he left," Robby said.

I nodded.

The color on the television shifted, became more muted and green, and the banner at the bottom of the screen blinked "LIVE." Robby and I sat on our couch and watched a funnel cloud form, heard the screams of the storm chasers as they filmed it. The camera switched to one in a helicopter, and as if we were God, we watched the tornado barrel through a town, rip apart homes and tear down trees that had been there for generations. It lifted up cars and lawn mowers and spit them out again. A dog ran from it, and Robby turned off the television so we wouldn't have to see what happened next.

"Unbelievable," he said.

"It's like the end of the world," I said, and I meant it. The earth felt full of energy, like it was gearing up for one grand finale. Our seasons had become more extreme in the last few years, floods followed by long droughts, blazing hot summers, winters entombed in ice for weeks at a time. It wasn't the Texas I'd grown up in, the one with the hot summers and mild falls and an occasional snow day every few years, and now with the tornadoes hitting daily first one town and then another, it felt like everything would soon be destroyed, our very own end of days.

"Speaking of the end of the world," I said. "I'm grabbing breakfast with my mom in the morning."

"Your favorite," he teased. I still saw my mother often, was still her everything. She was so proud of what I was doing with my life, that I was getting a doctorate and trying to become a professor. She acted like it was her own success, my drive and academic accomplishment, and even though I hated to admit it, I suppose it was, since she was the one who sacrificed her life and her dreams to raise a child.

Another storm rolled through that night, after Robby and I had gone to bed. It came out of nowhere, surprising even our best meteorologists. "Help me with the windows," Robby yelled, and we ran to shut them, our house as bright as day in the flashes of lightning. We mopped rainwater off the hardwood floors, stuffed towels in front of our leaking door jams. When the house was secure we huddled together in bed together, Robby and I, and we listened to the wind and the rain and the hail pounding on our windows, ripping through our roof.

My mother and I had a place we usually met for breakfast, a little diner we loved with oversized pancakes and bitter coffee, halfway between our homes, but it had been destroyed a few weeks ago. We talked of finding a new breakfast spot, but neither one of us was ready, so we met at the diner anyway, two of its walls blown away, booths broken and scattered, chairs toppled, counter crumbling. We brought muffins and coffee from a drive-through and ate them while we walked the damaged streets.

"Tell me everything, Claire," said my mother. "I've missed you so much. How are your exam preparations?"

Thank goodness for my exams, I thought. I wasn't ready to tell her about Josh yet. I had to see him first, find out for sure how he was, what type of role he would play in my life now that he'd reappeared.

"They're coming along fine," I lied. "Just a waiting game now."

I threw part of my muffin toward a couple stray dogs, who snarled at each other and licked the crumbs from the street. The animal shelters were overflowing, so many dislocated pups roamed the streets looking for their owners.

The truth about my exams was I wasn't ready, but my mom didn't need to know that. They were only three weeks away, and my house had become a dungeon of books and notes, dictionaries and encyclopedias and journals piled dozens deep on every surface. Robby waded through them when he came home from work, shuffled stacks around so he would have a place to sit at the table or a place to put his briefcase. I was specializing in Mexican-American literature. I wasn't Chicana, but there was something about it, some underlying sense of loss or separation, that drew me to the genre. I didn't know what I was doing when I picked that field, didn't know if I could pass, not as Chicana, which I clearly couldn't, but as a scholar. It felt like trying to get into a club I hadn't been invited to, a club with more trauma in its collective history than I could ever imagine. Every day I wrote out sample questions and read essays from students who had already passed and highlighted and outlined and summarized. Robby cooked for us most nights, or we ordered food in, and when he asked to go out to see a movie or a show, I had one response: "Anything after my exams." I would be glad when they were over.

I threw the rest of my muffin at the strays. "You need to stop doing that," said my mother. "They'll attack you."

"I just feel bad for them," I said. I imagined what it would have been like for them, those fifteen seconds that destroyed their worlds, when whatever fence or room kept them safe was lifted away to the winds and the world became suddenly too big.

"I hope you know how proud I am of you," said my mother, and she reached out and took my hand. I let her hold it, and I did my best not to flinch or let it show how hard I was trying not to pull back, and for me that was the greatest kindness I could offer her. After Josh left my whole body had been raw with his absence, and human touch, what was supposed to be the most healing thing in the world, felt like the worst kind of pain. I'd gotten better, but my mother's touch still felt like reopening a barely healed wound.

"I know, Mom," I said. "Thanks."

"Let's just hope the storms stay far away from you until you've passed," she said.

"Amen to that," I said, and I swallowed a sip of coffee.

I drove home from breakfast and listened to the radio dishing out stories of towns that had been destroyed, pets that had been found curled up next to dead owners, grandparents who'd had to leave the homes they built together as newlyweds, and I swerved to avoid felled trees and passed trucks loaded to the brim with family possessions, their owners evacuating before the storms could reach them, and I thought of Josh and how quickly he'd been taken from me before and could be taken again.

I'd planned to wait until after my exams to really and truly let him back into my life, but three weeks was too long. Something in seeing my mother, driving through so many destroyed towns, listening about the destruction of more on the radio made me anxious to see him immediately. I heard Robby in my head, listing the reasons and warnings, like what if Josh didn't really want to see me and forcing things like that made him shut me out entirely? Or what if a tornado struck while I was driving so far and my car was blown off an overpass? Or what if I got so caught up in Josh that I failed my exams? I hushed him and dialed the number I'd saved on my phone.

"Hey sis," he said.

"Hi, bud. I'm out your way, and I thought maybe I'd swing by and see you." I wasn't really out his way, but I was out at least. Only half of a lie.

"It's about time," he said.

Josh lived out in East Texas, where the pine trees grow tall, and the towns are small and isolated. His grandpa was a truck driver, so he and his grandma spent most of their time alone. He'd grown up in a doublewide on a few acres of land, pretty land, but unfriendly, cold in the winter and hot in the summer, filled with thorns and mosquitoes and wild hogs. His grandmother was nearly 80 and often sick now.

I'd seen pictures of Josh, and I'd talked to him, but I still wondered what he'd be like. There was a safety in not knowing for sure.

Josh was standing outside the trailer when I pulled onto the land, dressed all in black despite the muggy spring, heavy boots, knife clipped onto his belt loop, thin arms and legs, well over six feet. He waved when he saw me, and I rolled down my window and waved back.

"Hi, sis," he said when I parked. He reached out to hug me. I fit under his armpit, and I'm not sure what I was expecting, surely not the blond-haired baby, but also not this tall boy who smelled of sweat and weed.

"It's wonderful to see you, Josh," I said.

He held out a cigarette, and I shook my head. He lit one for himself and led me to his grandma's garage.

"Want to hear me play?" he said.

He pulled out an old beat-up guitar and started to strum, cigarette between his teeth, sweat stains on his shirt. He played all the artists a kid from Texas would know—Willie Nelson and Robert Earl Keen and Townes Van Zandt—and I sang along, no introductions, no small talk, just picking up where we left off back when he was small, as best we could, back when I used to get him dressed in the morning and sing him "Happy Together," and he'd sing with me when we came to the chorus and wiggle his diapered butt.

The first time Josh was arrested, he told me later that afternoon, he'd been ten and had attacked his teacher with a chair and been charged with aggravated assault. The next time he had stolen his grandmother's truck. The third time he'd been caught carrying a firearm into a movie theater. "Just for protection," he told me, and he opened a drawer and pulled out a Glock. I jumped back.

"Never seen a gun before?" he laughed, and showed me it wasn't loaded. He hadn't been to school in weeks. "My Nana's sick a lot," he said. "She tries to make me go to school, but I'm bigger than her, so what can she do?"

"You've got to want it yourself," I said.

"Nah, I'm over that shit," said Josh.

He was bipolar, off and on his medication depending on who was watching him. I asked him about social workers, since it seemed like a boy who'd been in jail six times would have people checking up on him. "They just make everything worse," he said, and he pulled off his leather jacket to show me his arms, scabbed and scarred by horizontal cuts.

I stared hard at him when he wasn't looking, trying to find hints of the baby I'd loved in this tough teenager. Some children grow up and look the same as they've always looked, but not Josh. His nose was the same, if I tried to see it, still small and slightly upturned. His eyes, too, the same bright blue they'd been when he was a baby. Other than that, I'm not sure I would have recognized him as my brother if I'd seen him on the street.

He wanted me to stay for dinner. His grandmother would be up from her nap soon, and he was putting some taquitos in the oven for her. I had promised Robby I'd be home in time to eat with him, though, so I asked for a rain check.

I hugged him again. "Call me, sis," he said, and I promised I would.

"Where have you been?" Robby asked. "I've been trying and trying to reach you."

"My phone's been off. I'm so sorry. But Robby, I met Josh today, went out to visit him. He lives out in East Texas with his grandma, you know, and he's so different, grown up, tough. It was weird, also really sad. I missed so much. I wish I'd been there for him."

"Claire, my parents got hit. A tornado. Have you been listening to the news? A big one went through their town."

Shit.

"They're fine, thank God, but lots of property damage." The tree he and his brothers had played on as kids had been ripped out, he told me, and parts of the roof had been torn off, which with the flash flooding could be bad.

"They need me to go help them nail a tarp down before all the rains come, but I didn't want to leave without knowing where you were."

"I'm sorry, Robby."

"Just next time leave your phone on?" he said, and I nodded.

"I'll be back late," he said. "Don't wait up."

He'd left dinner for me on the stove, a big pot of chili that was perfect after my long day. He was too good a man, always thinking of me even when I wasn't thinking of him. I ate and swallowed the guilt in each bite. After dinner I pulled out my books and studied at the kitchen table. The air outside was still, and the crickets chirped, and the streetlights shone through our windows.

I joined Robby at his parents' house early Saturday morning. His siblings would be coming too, and together we'd get as much cleanup done as we could. I'd told Josh about the damage—we'd been talking a lot—and he'd wanted to come help, but Robby wanted to keep it to just family. "I mean my family," he'd corrected himself. "And you, of course. I want to meet Josh, I really do, but there'll be time for that later."

"You're right," I'd said. "Okay."

Robby had grown up just outside the city. It had been mostly empty land when he was a boy, pastures of cows, fields of hay. Now it was filled in and suburban, but Robby's parents held onto their few acres of land, carved out their own semblance of country life while the city grew around them.

Robby's mother was in the kitchen when we got there. I hardly ever saw her out of it. She was frying a pan of bacon, scrambling some eggs, toasting slices of bread. "I thought you kids needed a good breakfast before you start working," she said. A couple of his siblings were there already, nieces and nephews running through hallways, in and out of doors. His family was loud and crowded. He was the middle child, with two older brothers and one younger and a baby sister right about my age. I didn't fit into their tribe, an only child with a single mother.

"Think you can give me a hand here?" his mother asked, and she handed me an apron and pointed to the pan of bacon. "Just keep an eye on that. Make sure it doesn't get too crunchy." I fumbled with the apron, winced when the bacon grease splattered on my arms.

"I've got it," Robby's sister, Bethany, said, and she took the spatula from me. "Maybe set out the orange juice?"

One of the older brothers had Robby in a headlock already, and their mother shooed them outside while we finished breakfast. "Those boys," she said and shook her head like she thought I understood.

My mother and I had eaten frozen dinners, picked a meal from our stack of lasagnas and enchiladas and battered fish to thaw each morning and eaten it that night in our rooms while we studied or worked or watched television. She was too busy paying the bills, and I living up to her expectations, to spend much time in the kitchen. After a few failed attempts at meals, I'd surrendered my kitchen to Robby, who cooked for both of us. I'm sure his mother wasn't crazy about this arrangement, but it worked for us.

Bethany and Robby's mother and I served breakfast to everyone else, the whole crowd of brothers and grandchildren, and then we got to work.

The damage was worse than we thought it would be, the backyard a pile of rubble, holes in the roof, paneling torn off the house. Robby and his brothers sawed off tree branches, and Bethany and I cleared away broken pieces of fence. The grandchildren helped with the lighter stuff or played together in the backyard. Their mothers had stayed home. The three brothers were giving them the day off from taking care of children, or maybe giving themselves the chance to be children again, I thought as I watched them swatting each other with sticks, pretending to lunge at each other with saws. I loved this big loud crowded family, but there was something about them that made me feel lonely, lonelier, at least, than when I was just with my mother.

"They'll always look like toddlers to me," said Robby's mother. We stood on the deck and watched the brothers hammer new boards into the fence. "It won't matter how old they are. I hope you get to know what that's like one day."

She set up lunch on the deck, a big long table, bread and deli meat and mustard and cheese. It was a cool and dry afternoon, summer heat still a few months away. A flock of sparrows chattered in one of the trees, and a woodpecker dipped from branch to branch. The siblings threw bread and condiments from one end of the table to the other. I'd reach out and grab at them when they passed me.

"How's that big test coming, Claire?" Robby's father asked. "We sure are proud of you."

"Gross, all that studying's not for me," said a brother.

"As if you needed to tell us that," answered another.

"It's fine," I said. "I'll be glad when it's over."

"First doctor in the family," Robby bragged.

"Not in the family quite yet," said his father. "When are you two going to make it official?" His wife swatted at him and warned him to leave us be. Robby was the only brother not yet married, although his sister was still single too. He brought it up sometimes. I wasn't ready. There was my degree to finish, and then the academic job search that would be grueling and could take me anywhere, and what was so bad about our life as it was?

"Take your time, sweetheart," said his mother. "There's no rush."

"Might be, with the earth going to hell and all," said the oldest brother.

"Never seen anything like it," said the father. "Not in all my life."

We were all sitting there, eating lunch, the brothers teasing each other, the children stuffing their mouths with food, when up walked Josh, same black jeans, shirt, and boots as before, dirtier now, sweatier, and a hammer hanging out of his belt loop.

"Hey, sis," he said. "I'm here to help."

Everyone turned to him. Robby's family was clean-cut, blue jeans and button-down shirts. Josh stood out, and so I stood out.

"This is my brother," I said. "My little brother, Joshua."

It took plenty of explaining. "You have a brother we've never met?" Robby's father said. "Come here, son. Shake my hand." Josh sneered a bit, and I thought that would be it, but then he held out his hand. Robby's mother looked Josh up and down, took in his wardrobe, his grease, his smell. His brothers nudged their children toward Josh, showed them the right way to greet a stranger.

"I told you not to come here," I said when at last I got Josh alone. "How'd you know where we were, anyway?"

"You told me Robby's name," he said. "I found his parents' address easy online. I wanted to help. I'm strong as fuck. You'll see."

I told him I'm sure he was, but that wasn't the issue. He'd showed up uninvited. There would be a time for him to meet Robby and Robby's family, but that time wasn't today.

"Well I'm here, sis," he said. "Might as well use me."

Robby joined us then, and I introduced him to Josh.

"So you're the boyfriend," said Josh. "You treating my sister all right?" Robby laughed. Josh's eyes narrowed. "I'm not shitting you," he said. "'Cause if you ain't, you've got me to deal with." He pulled his shirt to the side to show the knife he had clipped to his belt. Robby stepped back.

"Josh!" I said. I jerked his shirt back down over his knife. "What the hell?"

"Claire, can I talk to you?" Robby asked.

"This is a mess," I said. "Josh, you need to leave. Robby, I'm sorry. Can we talk later, though?"

"Who's leaving?" said Robby's dad. "No way. We can use all the help we can get." Robby protested, tried to explain what was going on, but his father wouldn't hear of it, and neither would Josh. And he was right, there was work to be done, and Josh was two more hands, if rather volatile ones.

It turned out fine, better than I'd expected. Once everyone got back to the cleanup, Josh fit right into the workforce. I watched him, passing branches from one brother to the other, joining them in their competition to see who was the strongest, sometimes even winning. Robby mostly ignored him, but the other boys joked around with him, put him in a headlock when he got too cocky, raced him to and from the street with armloads of debris. My family and Robby's family, all together. With Josh around, it wasn't just me and all of them. I had people.

We worked late that day. There was so much to do. By the time we left, the yard had been cleared and the fence mended and the roof patched. Robby's mother sent us all home with leftover food, cookies she'd baked and some spare avocados and tomatoes. "Your father and I can't eat everything before it goes bad," she said. "Look at this yard. What would we ever do without you kids?"

We had to drive Robby back to his trailer. He'd taken the bus over, and I didn't want to send him back on it. Robby said nothing all the way out there, and after I'd said goodbye to Josh, told him I appreciated his help but never pull a stunt like that again, nothing all the way back.

"I'm sorry, Robby," I said. "He just wanted to be with me. It's different for us than it is for you."

"I don't really want to talk about it," Robby said.

"Did you sleep at all last night?" Robby asked the next morning. I'd slept a little, but not much.

"We'll see how studying goes today," I said. I poured myself a cup of coffee, grabbed a banana and smeared almond butter on it.

"Should we talk about yesterday?"

"Not now." I swallowed some coffee, kissed him, grabbed my laptop and a copy of *George Washington Gomez* and went to the back porch to study. The air was heavy and thick, another storm brewing, although it likely wouldn't hit for another day or two. When I was a little girl I used to run outside when the sky turned green and the tornado sirens blared. I'd stand in the backyard and feel the wind, stronger and stronger around me, and when it was strong enough, I'd climb onto my swing set and hang from the monkey bars and let the wind blow me horizontal. No one would come looking for me, not in those long afternoons I'd spent home alone while my mother worked, no one to yell at me to get inside and under a mattress at once, no one to warn me how foolish I was being, how unthoughtful. Now I wondered where that bravery went, that foolhardy assurance that all would be fine, that I could let the storm blow my body any way it willed, delight in the feel of my own smallness against its power, and never once be in real danger.

The storms let up for a whole week. I spent my time studying, eating meals with Robby, talking to Josh on the phone. He called every morning and every night, texted throughout the day. Most of the time his texts just read, "Hey," and if I didn't reply he'd keep resending them. Every so often there'd be a stronger cry for connection, though: "Home alone with a loaded gun, trying to make a decision. Call me, sis."

I ended up talking to him all night long more than once, propped up on my elbows on our bed, feet in the air, like I was a teenager again, like Josh was still a baby falling asleep in the next room. Robby would come in, maybe tug on my toe. "Bedtime?" he would ask, and I'd whisper just a minute and move to the living room so he could go to sleep. Josh would sing me songs, and he'd tell me about how tomorrow he was going to take his grandma's truck and pick up his pregnant friend and her boyfriend, who were homeless and out of money, or we would talk about his parole and how if he didn't make it back to school one of these days he'd end up in Juvie again. I would try to hang up a couple times, but he'd always find some new reason to keep me on the line, and it was kind of nice, feeling needed, feeling connected, like I had back when he was small and he cried for me at night and I came in bleary-eyed and picked him up and brought him to my bed so we could both get some sleep.

I drove out to East Texas to see him a couple more times, always during the day when Robby was working. The drive was easier after a few days' reprieve from the storms, enough time for the county to come do some cleanup. When I was there we'd talk and play the guitar together. He was teaching me some chords. Sometimes he'd scowl when I mentioned Robby or said I really needed to get back to studying, maybe yell a bit, or smash his hand against the garage wall. He had a temper, but he usually kept it in check. Most of the time he was sweet, though, loving, grateful for the attention his grandmother wasn't giving him anymore.

"Can I ask you something?" Robby asked one night after I hung up the phone. "If you loved Josh so much, why didn't you stay in touch?" I knew what he was thinking, that if I'd stayed in touch we wouldn't be in this situation, trying to figure out our relationship with this new third wheel.

I'd seen Josh a few times, after he'd left. The first time his grandmother had cut his hair, all those long, beautiful curls I'd let grow. "Everyone thought he was a girl," she said. He was dressed in a NASCAR shirt, a brand new pair of cowboy boots. "We're going to change his last name to ours too, instead of his dad's. That way he'll be a Desmond like his momma," she said. "Hope that don't offend you."

The next time he had a black eye from fighting at preschool. "We told him if someone picks on him, he should give it right back to them," said his grandmother.

I was finishing up high school then, applying for colleges. Josh knew who I was, but he didn't remember his old room, didn't remember all the nights I'd sat in there with him singing him through thunderstorms, all the mornings I'd rubbed his back to wake him up, held him and rocked him until he could open his eyes and lift his head. By then when I sang him "Happy Together," he didn't sing back to me, had already forgotten our old routine. Then I left for college, and then I started grad school, and who can ever explain, really, why we fall out of touch with the ones we love the most?

"I don't really know," I told Robby. "I'm just glad to have him back now."

"Well just be careful, okay Claire?" he said. "Set some boundaries."

"He's just lonely, Robby. He doesn't have anyone."

"I know that, and I feel bad for him, but this whole thing gives me a bad feeling. He's asking a lot from you, from us, even though he knows you have your exams in a couple weeks, and he's pretty unstable. Just be careful."

I closed the book I'd had propped open and stood up. "He's just asking for time. He's been alone for years. It's the least I can give."

"It's not just time, though, is it?" said Robby. "He's asking a lot from you emotionally too." He said Josh was changing me, the way he was making me remember so much.

"I can't believe you, Robby," I said. "You have four brothers and sisters, and I've never once begrudged you the time your family demands."

"It's not the same thing, Claire. You know that. I'm happy you have him back. I'm just saying don't let him take over your life."

"Got it," I said, and I went to my bedroom to finish studying.

The thing is, I knew what he meant. I'd felt it too, that Josh wasn't the sweaty-headed baby I'd raised but some strange mentally ill fifteen-year-old boy, no more connected to me than any troubled sophomore in any high school in Texas. It was painful, seeing him now compared to how I remembered him. He wasn't improving my life, or my relationship with Robby. And then when I came close to hanging up the phone, ignoring a text message, telling him I didn't have time to drive to East Texas to visit, he'd say something, sing a line of a song, bring up some faraway memory I was sure he'd forgotten, and he'd be a toddler again, and I couldn't resist.

When the tornadoes returned they hit hard. They gave no warning, no gentle rain that grew to a storm. They blew cars off bridges and bulldozed through neighborhoods, broke windows, peeled walls off of homes. So many of our neighbors had returned during the reprieve, certain that the worst was over, that the world wasn't really about to end. Now they stood together in front of their crumbling houses and helped one another nail tarps over the roofs or carry out as many belongings as possible before the looters came.

A bad one hit only a few streets over from our home. Even though I'd been around tornadoes my whole life, that was something I never got used to, how one street could be flattened and the next one over still pristine. My mother called when she saw it on the news. I told her we were fine, it never even touched us, and besides, Robby was always careful about making us go to the storm cellar when any tornado popped on the weather radar. We knew what to do.

"Did you hear about those bad ones they had in East Texas?" she asked.

"What? Where?"

She told me she'd seen them on the news. Robby and I must have been in the cellar and not heard. The storms had demolished a few East Texas towns, lots of fatalities, lots of property damage, electricity down too.

I turned on the news and watched the footage. I recognized some of the landmarks from my visits to see Josh, the big water tower, the courthouse in the middle of town, a little white chapel with stained glass. The footage showed houses leveled flat, dogs curled up beside dead owners, lakes clogged with debris.

I tried calling Josh again and again, but no one answered. "The cell phone towers must be down," Robby said.

"I have to know he's okay." I thought of his trailer, and how tornadoes can sneak up without warning, certainly without enough to make it to the nearest storm cellar.

Robby grabbed his keys. "Let's go check," he said, and I remembered why I loved him so much.

The destruction was worse than the news showed. A few of the stronger houses were still standing, but most people in Josh's town lived in trailers or small wooden homes that had been swept up in the wind. I drove us to Josh's land. The trailer was gone, most of the trees on the property torn up from their roots. We bounced over broken branches and fence posts, and I pulled in to park.

"Doesn't look good," Robby said.

"Please don't." I called Josh again and again, left message after message. Josh wasn't the type to let his phone go to voicemail. He answered after the first ring, sometimes even before, ever eager for the attention he knew was on the other end.

The sky was deep East Texas blue, and cardinals sang in the broken branches. There'd been rain most of the night, but now the storms were past. A stray dog wandered onto the property and came up to us looking for food. We pet it, gave it some water from our bottles and a few bites of a granola bar.

"I'm sorry, Claire. We'll find him, okay?" Robby said. He suggested we look at a missing persons list.

"Good idea," I said, and so we got back in the car and drove to the police station, where photos of dead or missing citizens papered the walls. We stared at every single picture, every single name, even went back and checked them all again, but we couldn't find Josh, or his grandmother.

It felt fitting, right somehow, that it would end this way. That Josh would be swept away in a storm, taken from me again right when I was getting him back. It felt like the only thing that could have happened.

"Can I help you two?" an officer asked. "You looking for someone?"

"Yes, ma'am," I said. "I'm looking for my little brother and his grandmother." I gave the officer their names.

"Oh, you mean the Desmonds? Yeah, I know them. Even arrested Josh a couple of times." She laughed, then she said their house had been completely destroyed. "They're staying up the road a ways with the Turners. Real good folk."

Robby had been holding my hand, and he gave it a little squeeze when we heard that Josh was fine. I got directions from the officer and thanked her.

The officer called to us as we were leaving.

"You're his sister, you said?"

"Yes, ma'am."

"Someone needs to keep an eye on that boy. He's trouble."

"Don't say anything," I told Robby while we drove.

"I wasn't going to," he said.

"The nerve of that woman."

"Claire," he said.

"Of course he's headed for trouble when everyone keeps telling him he is. How about instead of arresting him you make sure he goes to school every day and takes his meds?"

"He's safe right now, so just think about that."

"He's a good kid, Robby. He really is." I told him about the sweet things Josh had done for me, like buy me lunch last time I came out even though he didn't make any money, or how when he hung up he always told me how much he loved me and was glad to have me back in his life, or how sometimes when his mind wandered and he forgot to be tough his eyes slipped back into what they had been, hopeful and sweet and gentle. "He's a good kid."

"We'll find him," said Robby.

Josh was there when we pulled into the Turners' drive. He ran to our car to greet us, gangly teenage frame clad in its customary heavy black jeans and black shirt.

"Hey, sis!" he said. "Were you worried about me?"

I hugged him tight, sweaty shirt and all, my little brother. "We've been looking everywhere," I said. He grinned.

"You gave us quite the scare, kid," Robby said, and stepped forward, hand outstretched.

I wasn't sure how Josh would react. After their last conversation, they'd spent the day cleaning Robby's parents' house together, lifted and cleared and hammered, and I thought they were good, but I couldn't be sure.

Josh took Robby's hand, though, shook it and said he was glad to see him.

"How about some lunch," Robby said. "My treat."

We went to a little buffet down the road, one of the few restaurants still standing, its parking lot filled with pickups, a line of patrons stretching out the door.

"Guess we're eating here," Robby said.

"This place is good. Best ribs in town. You'll like it," said Josh.

We piled our trays with barbeque and chicken fried steak and potato salad and rolls, filled our glasses with sweet tea, found a booth for all three of us.

"Now this is what I call a meal," said Josh.

Robby laughed. "To be young again," he said.

"Tell me the best thing you ever had to eat," Josh said, and Robby told us about the Thanksgiving meals his mother used to make, how she would spend weeks baking pies, sometimes ten or fifteen of them. After dinner they'd line the pies up on the counter and taste them all.

"We'd eat pie for days," he said. I'd never baked a pie. Marie Callender's was my best friend over the holiday, although Robby usually made a couple from scratch. "How about you, Claire?"

I thought of the meals Robby had cooked for me, truly the best I'd ever eaten, the way he could sear a steak to perfection, top it with béarnaise sauce or mushrooms. There were a few remarkable restaurant dinners, nights either he or my mother had taken me out to celebrate.

"That's easy," I said. "The best meal I ever had was fourteen years ago. You were turning one, and I took you to McDonald's to celebrate. You'd never been before. I bought you a cheeseburger and an ice cream cone. You didn't know what it was, but you got the hang of it pretty fast." It had dripped down his face, all over his shirt. His curls were sticky with ketchup and smashed hamburger meat. After he'd eaten I'd taken him to the playground and helped him go down the slide, and he'd laughed so hard I thought he'd choke. When he hit the bottom, he ran to me, put his arms around my neck, his sticky mouth against my ear, and given me the most disgusting kiss I'd ever received. "We were so happy together that day," I said. "I've never tasted food like that again."

"Ouch," said Robby.

"Sorry," I said. "Your meals are good too."

"Gross, sis," said Josh. We were all three laughing, Josh and Robby and me. It felt good, right.

"I sure could use some pie now," said Josh.

"Me too," said Robby, and the two of them got up and went back to the buffet. I watched them together. They were getting along. Robby was going to be so good for Josh, I thought.

They came back with apple and peach and chocolate. We all tried bites of all three, but we agreed the chocolate was the best. Fruit pies just needed to be homemade, Robby said, and he was probably right. Josh got us all another round of chocolate. I don't remember the last time I ate so much, not since I was a little kid probably, stuffing myself without any fear of the consequences the way only little kids know how to do. Robby and Josh were onto sports. It was basketball season, and they were arguing over whether the Spurs or the Mavs were the better team.

"Maybe I can take you to a game sometime this spring," said Robby.

"Sure, dude, I'd like that," Josh said. I laughed at his tough nonchalance, no mask for his real excitement.

"This was fun," said Josh. "Y'all should come out more often."

"Of course we will," I said.

Josh sat in the back on the ride back to the Turners' house, Robby and I in the front. We made a good family, I thought, and I pictured all the times we would be sitting like this, on our way to basketball games or dinners out or maybe someday Josh's graduation.

Back at the Turners' Josh thanked us again.

"Seriously, I had a great time," he said.

"No problem, buddy. We had a good time too," said Robby.

"Hey, you think before you leave you could lend me some money? It'd just be such a help while my grandma and me are trying to get back on our feet."

Robby looked at me. I jumped in.

"I don't know about that, Josh," I said. "We can come out and help you, though. Or take you shopping?"

"What? You don't trust me?"

"It's not that, sweetie. It's just."

"Just that he doesn't trust me," Josh looked at Robby.

"Of course he does. He loves you."

"Don't you lie to me, sis."

Robby stepped in then. "Of course we trust you, Josh. We'll help you in any way we can."

"Except giving me money. Real winner you picked here, Claire."

"Come on, Josh," I said. "Robby really cares for you. He helped me look for you all day. It was his even idea to come out here."

I saw the hurt flash across his eyes.

"It wasn't your idea, sis?"

"I mean, it would have been. Robby just thought of it first. You're important to him."

"Just not to you."

"Calm down there, buddy," Robby said.

"Why don't you just stay out of this? You've done enough already," said Josh.

"Josh, you can't talk to him like that," I said.

"It's okay, Claire," said Robby. "Maybe I'll just wait in the car."

"What, too pussy to talk to me?"

"Okay, Josh, simmer down," I said. "Robby's one of the good ones."

"He'd better be." He turned back to Robby. "Wanna know how many ways there are to kill a man?" he said.

"Josh!" I said.

"First you could crush his throat. That's real easy to do. You could smother his mouth and nose, bash his head, stab his chest, or of course poison him, but that's for pussies."

I cut him off. "That's enough."

Robby was done being nice by then. "He's a real charmer, Claire," he said. "I can see why you love him so much."

"Robby, come on."

"You got something to say, say it to me," said Josh.

"Josh," I said. "Okay guys, something went way wrong here. Let's just start over." I reintroduced them to each other, mocked cheer and warmth. They were facing each other by then, though, neither one paying much attention to me.

"I'm serious," said Josh. "I take care of my own."

"I'll bet you do," said Robby, and he turned back toward me. "Claire, I'll be in the car. When you're done with this little punk, just let me know."

"That's how you talk to her?" said Josh. "You think you can just boss her around like that?"

"Look man, Claire's right. We got on the wrong foot somehow. I came here to help, not fight. Claire wants us to get along. We're both important to her."

"I know I am. I'm her brother. You're just some dude she's fucking. I've been with ten girls already this year."

"Not sure I'd brag about that," Robby muttered, under his breath, but still too loudly.

Josh swung, and his fist hit Robby's nose.

"Shit," Robby yelled. He lunged at Josh. He had three brothers, was used to swinging back. He could pull his weight if he needed to, but I could see he was restraining himself, taking more than he gave. I was right in there with them, grabbing at their shirts, yelling at them to stop.

By then Josh's grandmother had come out. She wore a flowered housedress and leaned on her walker. She napped most afternoons, and I'd only spoken to her a few times, when I was coming or going from visiting Josh, or when she asked Josh to put me on the line so she could say hi to me while we were talking.

"Josh? What's going on?" she said

Josh and Robby stopped and looked up at her, and I tried to explain the situation.

His grandmother interrupted me. "Josh, you know you can't keep fighting like this," she said. "They'll put you back in jail."

Josh glared at Robby.

"Look man, no hard feelings," said Robby. "Things just got really out of hand."

Josh nodded and backed away.

"We just wanted to make sure both of you were okay," I told Josh and his grandmother. "Sorry to cause all this trouble. We'll leave you now."

"Wait, sis," said Josh. "Wanna hear some more of my music? I've been practicing lots lately."

"Seriously?" Robby said, low enough that only I could hear him.

"I'd love to, Josh, but it'll have to wait," I said. "Another time."

Robby was quiet on the way home, just held his bloody nose and looked out the window while I drove. "He's had a hard life," I said. "He doesn't have any good male role models." Robby said nothing. "I'll make sure to talk to him and explain how much I want you two to like each other," I said. Still nothing. After a while I stopped talking too, and we drove the rest of the way in silence.

I helped him clean his nose later that night, cooked him dinner, declined his offer to help wash dishes afterward. "I really am sorry," I said a few times, and he'd shrug and tell me not to worry about it, that we didn't get to choose our family, it wasn't my fault, although I knew he didn't mean any of it. My mom stopped by after dinner.

"I thought I'd surprise you," she said. "Bring you some meals while you're busy studying." Plastic shopping bags hung from her arms, filled with frozen lasagnas and enchiladas and breaded fish.

"You shouldn't have, Mom," I said, and reached out to help her with the groceries. I motioned to Robby to hide his nose, which had swollen up and was still bleeding a little, but it was too late.

"Robby, what happened to you?" she asked him. He started to cover for me, tell my mom he'd been wrestling with his brothers or something, but I interrupted him.

"It was Josh," I said.

"Josh who?"

"Josh my brother. Remember him?" I waited for a second. "He's back."

"What do you mean he's back?" she asked.

I told her how he'd found me online and we'd gotten back in touch, how it started with phone calls and texts, but now I'd been visiting him a few times a week.

"And Robby's nose?" she asked, so we told her about the morning and Josh and Robby's fight.

"It's not as bad as it sounds," I said.

"Claire, can I talk to you?" she asked. "Alone?"

I led her to the back porch. I knew everything she was about to say, how she would warn me about letting him in, especially now, tell me I owed him nothing, he wasn't my real brother, had never truly been.

Once upon a time I'd begged her to let us adopt him. I was fifteen, almost sixteen. I told her if we adopted him I'd never ask for another thing as long as I lived, no sweet sixteen party, or expensive presents, no car for graduation, no trip to Europe in college. I'd told her she'd never have to worry about him. He would be my responsibility. She would raise me, and I'd raise Josh.

He was nearly two then. To prove to my mom that I could handle the responsibility of a brother I'd taken a job at Josh's daycare center after school. It came with a tuition drop for him, which benefited my mother, and it gave me an extra few hours a day with Josh. I was assigned to the preschoolers, and Josh was in the toddler room, but he always knew exactly when I arrived, somehow. He'd pound at the door of his room, screaming, crying my name. "Taire," he called me, and I'd hear it down the hall, over and over. After a few minutes, his teachers always brought him to me, and he'd sit in my lap, his head against my chest, while I taught the four-year-olds. "Aren't there other jobs you want?" my mother would ask. She wanted me to get new experiences, figure out what I wanted for my life, but I already knew.

We could have had permanent custody of him. That was the hardest part for years, that he could have been ours forever. His mother was uninterested, and his grandmother was too old to raise a child. I could have been his mother, my own mother his grandmother. It's what I asked for, what I wanted more than anything in the world. "But I want more for you than that," my mother had said. "I don't want you to be a teen mom, and you know I can't raise him, not when I'm working so many hours already." It was her greatest fear, that my life would become what hers had, that I'd be cursed with my own version of me, never mind that without me she would be all alone. So she sent him away to his grandmother, where they cut his hair and changed his name. And that's why I never forgave her.

"We have to talk about this, honey," she said. But there wasn't anything to talk about, and I told her that. It was done, Josh was back, I loved him and wouldn't let him go again. He needed me, like I had needed her.

"How is he? We haven't seen him in what, ten years?"

I told her about jail, and how he hadn't been to school in months, about his sick grandmother and the way he was raising himself, prone to mood swings and violence. I spared nothing. I wanted her to know the full cost of her abandonment.

"Claire," she said. "Honey. Are you sure this is the right time for this, with your exams so close? I've, we've, sacrificed so much for you to get where you are. You're risking it all on this boy, a stranger to you, really. You don't owe him anything."

"I knew you'd say all that," I said. "You've never once understood."

"That's not fair," she said. "I just want what's best for you."

"Josh is what's best for me. He always has been."

At last the morning of my written exams arrived. I didn't feel ready for them, but I wanted them over, wanted whatever was on the other side to arrive. I hoped the tension between Robby and me would be gone then, that maybe our other problems would go away once this big hurdle was cleared. We'd been speaking, but barely: "hellos" and "goodbyes," "what time will you be home?" and "can I pour you another cup of coffee?" Robby's father always said that sometimes love just means having good manners, and there was something to that, but I wanted more than manners, wanted him to understand, to embrace my little brother the way I had, invite him to our home, maybe even permanently, and manners couldn't get us to that point.

Things with Josh were good, though, better than good. I spent almost every day out in East Texas with him. I was helping him and his grandmother move into their new trailer. It was smaller than their old one, not really new, of course, but Josh was excited about settling into his bedroom. I took him shopping, bought him a new bedspread and desk. "This way when you go back to school you'll have a place to study," I said, and winked at him. I'd find a way to make him go soon, once our relationship was strong enough. I bought him notebooks and pencils, the things he would need once he went back, and while we were shopping he asked me for a new guitar case, his old one couldn't protect the guitar his grandfather had passed down to him years ago, and so I bought it, the nicest one in the store. "Where is all this money coming from?" Robby asked. "You're a graduate student."

"I haven't bought him things in ten years," I said. "It evens out."

The day before my tests began I had lunch with Josh and explained that I wouldn't be available for a couple days. I bought him everything he wanted to eat, watched as he slurped up Dr. Pepper and swallowed two brisket sandwiches and potato salad. I didn't want him hungry when I told him the news.

"It'll just be two days, but for those two days I won't be able to talk," I said. "No phone calls, no texts. I can't be distracted."

"What if there's an emergency?" Josh said, and washed down a chunk of brisket with Dr. Pepper. "What if I need you?"

"You'll have to wait. You can do without me for two days, buddy. You're fifteen."

I hated saying it. He'd done without me for ten years, ten years when he wasn't fifteen, when he was just a child, alone and neglected with an ailing grandmother.

"Okay, sis," he said. "Two days."

The day of my exams Robby made me breakfast and brewed a pot of coffee that I could drink for hours. We ate bacon and eggs and strawberries, spread butter thick on English muffins, drank strong coffee, talked very little. "You've got this," Robby said once, and I nodded, smiled at him a little, and ate.

My committee would email me my questions at 10 a.m., and I'd have two days to write as much as I could. The following week I would go into the university for my oral defense, where they'd question me on what I wrote, ask me about the holes in my argument, or places it needed expanding. I would have a lot of those, I knew, but hopefully not so many that I wouldn't pass. Another storm was forecasted for the afternoon, and the air was heavy and thick and waiting. I hoped it would hold off for a couple of days, since a bad storm could cause electricity blackouts.

"What will you do if Josh calls?" Robby asked.

"He won't."

Robby nodded like he didn't believe me, like he didn't think I believed myself either, and I cleared the table from breakfast and poured another cup of coffee.

My first question was about code-switching in literature, asking me to analyze what it does to the text, how the presence of two languages melded into one creates a universe unique and isolated and specific to that text alone. It was a question that excited me, although I hadn't grown up bilingual, because it stretched beyond Latinx literature, because who hasn't experienced that deep bond that people can have when they find the ones who are most like themselves, the way they separate from the rest of the world, create their own isolated communities, with their own speech and values and customs?

I thought of Josh while I was writing, how over the past few months our ways of speaking had become our own, how I could hear "Hey, sis" over the phone and know in a second what it meant.

I was writing on a deadline, so I worked quickly, took few breaks, but I still found it peaceful, almost relaxing. I loved feeling focused and free of distraction. My life lately had been so blurred, Josh's constant need for me, the growing static between Robby and me, all the tornadoes and their impending doom.

But for two days, nothing mattered except these questions, questions that felt important, as a scholar, but probably weren't. They wouldn't save the world, wouldn't solve anything. They wouldn't return Josh to me as a toddler, give me back all those years so I could watch him grow up and protect him. They wouldn't keep him out of jail or make him go to school. They wouldn't make Josh and Robby friends, or help Robby and me finally talk to each other. They weren't even supposed to. There was something peaceful in their futility. It felt like hiding away for a couple days, like finding a cabin high up on a mountainside and staying there and pretending the world and its problems no longer existed.

That night Robby made dinner. He wanted us to relax, drink wine, go for a walk, but this was only a pause, not the end. I had to do it all again tomorrow, and then I had my defense. Josh had texted over a dozen times during the day. I'd expected that. Not calling would be hard enough for him. Asking him not to text was too much. So Robby cleaned up from dinner and I read Josh's texts and called him back.

"I learned how to play a new song," he said. "Listen, sis." He played me "Folsom Prison," even plucked out the base line on his guitar. It was our own language, me with the phone pressed to my ear, Josh on the other end strumming some country song. We were becoming our own world, maybe the way we always should have been.

"Remember I've got another day of testing tomorrow, Josh," I said when he finished playing.

"You sure?" he said. "Today took forever."

"It wouldn't seem so long if you'd just go back to school," I said.
"Yeah, I know."
"One more day, little brother. You got this."

The second day of my exams the storm still hadn't come, although
I could feel in the air they were nearby. I hoped they would hold out
throughout the day and then let loose in the evening, after the last of
my exams had been turned in and I had nothing to do, when Robby
and I could open a bottle of wine and curl up on the couch and listen
to the thunder and wind and rain. The second day was easier than the
first. I wasn't prepared, but my answers came naturally. There was a
reason I'd devoted so many years to graduate school. This was what I
was good at. I could try to change the world as much as I wanted, but
when it came right down to it, the thing I was best at was sitting alone
in a room writing essays about the ways postcolonial theory shows
up in Mexican-American literature. It was depressing really, but also
calming, like surrender.

By the time I finished, the sun was filtering light through an
emerald sheen, the wind sweeping the humidity out of the air. Robby
was waiting for me on the back porch, confetti and party hats ready,
and when I opened the screen door and shouted, "I finished," he
covered me with colored paper and put a plastic crown on my head
and kissed me on the mouth.

"I should call Josh," I said.

"Just wait," he said, and he pulled me to him and turned on the
radio and we danced and laughed like we hadn't in at least three
weeks, the crown slipping down over one eye, the confetti falling at
our feet.

"I've missed this," he said. "Us."

"Me too."

"Wait and call Josh tomorrow."

I started to say no. I knew I'd have messages from Josh, that he'd
want to know I hadn't forgotten him while I was testing, but Robby

was smiling at me and kissing behind my ear, and my written exams were over and I had a whole week before my oral defense, a whole week to relax and unwind after the past year of studying, the past three weeks of Josh. He'd be fine for one night.

The thunder cracked then, the first peal of the night, without any warning. We must have missed the lightning while we were dancing, laughing. And the rain started, heavy and loud, and the neighbor's wind chimes blew their frantic thunderstorm song, and the branches on the old pecan tree in our front yard rattled against each other. I pulled Robby inside, onto the sofa, where the rain fell on us through the open window, and it was just the two of us, and we were happy.

We fell asleep there, curled around each other listening to the storm. I dreamed of babies born too early to parents too young. Of newborns shaking drugs out of their bodies. Of brothers and sisters pulled apart forever. Of jails filled with lost children.

I woke up early and knew something was wrong, felt it in my skin and my hair and my teeth. The carpet was soaked from the storm. It had felt romantic to let the rain blow in on us the night before, but now we'd have to dry it before it mildewed. I untwisted myself from Robby and slid off the couch. It felt like the world must have been destroyed, that something in my body was telling me what we had feared had finally happened. I went to the window to check the damage. Outside was no worse than after any storm, though, some fallen branches, a few shingles blown off, nothing more.

I remembered Josh then and checked my phone. There were over a hundred messages from him, too many to listen to or read, but the last few all said that he needed me to meet him at the hospital right away.

"I have to go," I said to Robby, who opened his eyes and looked up at me. "Josh is hurt."

Josh had told me what hospital he'd be at, and I drove straight there. The parking lot was full, too many patients with so many tornadoes, so I parked far away and ran. Josh and his grandmother were by the front desk checking out, Josh in crutches, a cast on his foot.

"Josh, honey, what happened?" I asked.

"Broken," he said. I asked him how, and he told me the story, how his parole officer had stopped by and said if he missed any more school he'd have to go back to Juvie, how after he'd left Josh started yelling at anyone who was around, his grandmother, the Turner kids, the dog, how the Turners had threatened to call the cops if Josh didn't calm down, how Josh had run outside and kicked a tree again and again until his toes were crooked and swelling.

"Better than hurting someone else," he said.

"Well, yeah, I guess," I said.

"And this way I get a pass from school for a couple days!"

"Can I talk to you?" Josh's grandmother grabbed my arm. She told Josh to wait at the desk and pulled me into the next room, where we could talk alone. "I just can't do this anymore," she said. "I'm too old to deal with him. Will you take over?"

I'd dreamed of her saying that so many times when I was a teenager. She'd finally come to her senses and realize what she'd gotten herself into, and I'd take Josh back. He'd be only four or five, still plenty of childhood left ahead of him, and I'd let his curls grow back, and I'd dress him in those little red Oshkosh overalls like the ones he'd worn as a baby, and it would be as if he never left.

Here it was happening at last, and I looked at Josh with his broken foot and crutches, his already long criminal record, his failing grades, his black shirt and boots and pants, the clip that usually held his knife empty since we were in a hospital, and I hated everything and everyone in this world.

"Of course I will," I said. "Josh is my brother. Just let me ask my boyfriend first."

Robby was waiting at home for me with another meal he'd cooked, another bottle of wine. "Ready for more celebrating?" he said. "Everything okay with Josh?"

"No," I said, and I told him everything that had happened and what his grandmother had asked. "She's just overwhelmed. I told her we could do it, as long as you agreed."

Robby put down the wine he was uncorking. "Do you have any idea what that would be like?" he said. "Raising a troubled teenager? He needs serious help, more than you or I can give him."

"I know that. But we can at least try. No one else is trying. He's my responsibility."

"But he's not. He's not your son, Claire. He's hardly even your brother."

"He should have been," I said.

I remember every detail from the day Josh left, a hot September morning back when I was sixteen. I still had to go to school. My mother wouldn't hear of me skipping no matter how hard I begged. Josh's grandmother came to get him early so that I could say goodbye before I left. I remember what toys he was playing with (a Fisher Price airplane), what he ate for breakfast (waffles), what he was wearing (denim shorts and an orange shirt and a backwards baseball cap). I didn't cry once that morning. I didn't want to do that to him. I sang him the songs he loved. We danced one last time to "Happy Together." I sang, but I couldn't look at him or I knew I'd break down.

"It's time," said my mother, and she put her hand on my shoulder. "You'll see him again." I remember the weight of him in my arms, how it felt cruel, that he could be mine until I put him in the car seat, but I wasn't free not to put him in—a twisted and malicious type of free will. I buckled him in and kissed his head one last time, and his grandmother drove him away.

"I can't agree to that, Claire, and I can't believe you'd tell his grandmother we could take him before you asked me."

"I'm asking you now," I said. "I was just sure you'd say yes."

"I can't help you raise Josh. I've tried to be understanding about this whole thing, but this is just too much."

"You can't have me without him, Robby. I thought you knew that. We're a packaged deal now."

"What if it were him or me?"

"Is it?"

I saw Robby deflate a little, pause.

"I'll tell you what," he said. "After your exams, what if Josh stays with us for a couple nights? Gets a little break from his grandmother? That's the most I can do."

"He doesn't need a vacation. He needs a home."

I visited Josh in East Texas every day that week. It was a two-hour drive, but I didn't mind making it twice daily to see him, to let him know that I was there for him now and always. It meant Robby and I hardly saw each other at all, and I was glad for that. I wondered if there was any difference between Robby and my mother, who both thought they knew what was best for me, both refused Josh for their sake and for mine. I didn't know what I would do if I really had to choose. Josh was my brother. Would it even be a choice?

Josh hobbled along on his crutches, sporting his cast—black, of course—for everyone to see. "This way they'll know not to mess with me," he'd say.

"He always did have a temper," my mother said when I told her about Josh's injury.

Josh's grandmother was disappointed when I told her we couldn't take Josh, but she said she understood Robby's reluctance. "He's a handful."

Was I the only one, I wondered, who saw everything he once was in him still? The only one who saw that crooked smirk that drove adults crazy and remembered the little grin from his childhood? The one who heard him crooning "Sunday Morning Coming Down" and remembered his voice lisping out nursery rhymes? His parole officer came to visit one day while I was there. "You the sister?" he asked, Josh and I sitting beneath a tall East Texas pine, strumming on guitars and singing Kris Kristofferson. "Josh has mentioned you. He's trouble, this one, huh?"

Josh and I made plans for his future during our afternoons in East Texas. He didn't share his grandmother's understanding of Robby, but I tried to help him see. "We both have lives, buddy, careers. But if you can get yourself back to school, stay out of trouble. You're a great kid, and as soon as Robby understands that I'm sure he'll let you live with us." Josh promised to try. "And no more fighting," I told him.

My oral defense had been scheduled for fairly late on a Thursday. I'd go in and be quizzed for two hours over what I wrote, asked to clarify, explain, expand, and then I would be a doctoral candidate. It was the last step before I switched my focus to my dissertation. One penultimate hurdle. During my defense the committee would give me suggestions about my dissertation, advise paths of research, recommend certain books to read and scholars to interview. I appreciated the chance to stay busy with Josh that week. There was little I could do to prepare for my oral defense, other than read my exams again and again and agonize over every word choice and example. Josh kept me from worrying. After my exams Josh would come to stay with us for two nights, Robby's concession. It wasn't much, but at least a start.

I'd bought new clothes, dress slacks and a blazer, a bleached white button down, the sort of white that makes other white look gray. I wore high black pumps, even though I usually wore comfortable flats to teach and tutor. Robby said he'd drop me off at the university so I didn't have to wobble the three quarters of a mile over pockmarked sidewalks. I'd practiced my make-up, blended just the right colors of eye shadow to make my eyes stand out without appearing juvenile. I skipped my normal streak of eyeliner and pulled my hair into a bun so that the gray that was beginning to grow underneath would show. The purpose of this defense was to transform me into my professors' peer, I'd been told, to prove that I could function as their equal, was deserving of their recommendations when I applied for professorship positions.

"Well I'd pass you," said Robby when I stepped out of the bathroom. I kissed him. "Once this is done, we'll celebrate?" he asked, his way of making sure I wasn't visiting Josh this evening.

"Yes," I said. "Exams passed and Josh coming to visit tomorrow. We'll definitely celebrate." I grabbed my purse and a folder with five hard copies of my written exams. "Ready," I said, and then my phone rang. I pulled it out of my purse. "It's Josh."

"Don't."

"He might need me."

"Claire, please don't." He reminded me of my exams in just half an hour, the years of work I'd put into this day, the way Josh had a way of derailing things. "You know whatever it is, it's not good news," he said.

"I'm sick of people believing the worst about him," I said. I answered the phone.

"Josh's voice was fast and breathless. I heard, "cops," "arrested," "help."

"Slow down, Sweetie," I said, and he explained. He'd stolen the Turners' car since it was hard to get around on crutches. They'd caught him backing out of the driveway. He hadn't even made it to the street, but on top of all the trouble Josh had already given him, they were pressing charges. The PO was on his way. "My grandma won't bail me out this time," he said. "If you don't come sign for me I'll go back to Juvie. "Help me sis," he said. "Now."

People talk of the ones that got away. Their high school boyfriends who got the best and most vulnerable parts of their hearts. Their missed connections that could have become so much more. Their first marriages that they were too young to save. My one that got away was a little boy with long blond curls and faded overalls, who clung to me like I was his mother, who deserved a better life than the one he got. When it comes down to it, he's the only person I've ever really loved.

"Don't go, Claire. Your exams. You can't save him. It's too late."

"I can." I would start at the beginning, I told him, remake Josh, from the outside in, with clothes and books and a nice haircut. I wouldn't let him go to school dressed in black, daring the other students. He would need extracurricular activities, maybe guitar lessons? Sports would be good, teach him how to work with people. Of course social workers would be involved, probation officers. There would be therapy sessions, doctors' appointments, medication.

"Then it's time to make a choice," Robby said.

"Robby, please."

"There's not room for us both." He held onto my hand, waited.

"He's my brother," I said.

The tornado came the next week, the one we'd all known would come. It tore through my university, flattened the conference room I should have been in the day Josh called. It broke the windows of the house, left shards of glass all over the bed that Robby and I had slept in for years. Josh was sleeping on the couch when the sirens sounded.

I heard the sirens and ran to Josh. I told him to come with me. Our neighbors had a storm cellar. Maybe Robby would find us there. I would be looking for him for a long time.

Josh grabbed his crutches and his guitar, followed me down the street, and I told myself again that it was good he was here and not in juvie, riding out the storm wherever they rode out storms in the detention center.

We waited there, in our neighbors' storm cellar, with as many people as would fit. There was Mrs. Baker from next door, who yelled at anyone who parked in front of her mailbox for even a few minutes. There was Mr. McDouglass, who had lost his wife to cancer years ago and now was more of a ghost story than a real flesh-and-blood person. There was Ms. Smith, who was raising two young children on her own for reasons no one else knew. There were others too, children and adults, a few dogs and cats, a couple of chickens.

And Josh. There he was, crutches propped against the wall, black cast and black jeans, although he hadn't bothered to grab a shirt. When the storms got bad he pulled out his guitar and started strumming. We sat there, all of us, and we listened to him play, and then someone joined in, and then another, and then we were all singing, singing all the old songs, Johnny Cash and Willie Nelson, and a bit of George Strait thrown in, while outside the wind blew hard and fast, and the trees cracked, and the violence swelled.

'TIL MORNING

It's late summer in London, and all of the pigeons have died. My sister and I sit beside the Thames and watch their bodies float down the river, lifeless and waterlogged and gray. Yesterday they filled the London sky, but something happened overnight, something that must have been terrible. I dip a finger in the river and twirl a bird around and around in a whirlpool until it disappears. I look at my sister and try to know what she is feeling.

We have been here all summer, my sister and I. She has just graduated from high school, and I from college, and we are seeing the world. Without pigeons, the London sky is emptier but just as gray. The river is thick and clogged. Boats push through the birds, and the bodies part. "What do you think happened?" I ask. My sister shrugs and says she doesn't know. She is unhappy here, on this vacation to Europe that so many would love to have. She is too young for this trip, and I wish I'd come alone. I feel her weight on this continent I want to discover, the way I have felt it my whole life.

Stuart meets us at the river. "Can you believe this?" he says, and he shakes his head at the bodies. I met him one night early this summer when I was taking the night train to Rome. The train was full, and my sister and I hadn't reserved a space beforehand and had to share our car with more and more passengers. There was a young man from Venice who was traveling to his brother's funeral, and a missionary from Nigeria who kept us awake all night with his preaching, and a woman from France who bought more candy to eat each time the concession cart rolled past, and the car was full of languages and sugar and sweat and exhaustion, and Stuart looked over everybody at me and rolled his eyes. For two months now we have been together, visiting museums and cafes and churches. I'm not good at dating, not more than a few months at least, and so Stuart is perfect. He shows me his city, and he keeps my sister from feeling guilty that she doesn't want to tour with me, and in one more week, long before we can grow comfortable enough with each other to turn mean, I will leave him behind and never see him again.

In London my sister and I buy bread and fruit to eat in our hotel. The room we have rented is small and crowded, barred windows that look out on a dirty street and hall mates who walk around naked and yell at each other through the night. "I miss Texas," says my sister, "especially now," and I remind her again that we only have a week left and we need to make the most of it. "I know that already. You don't need to keep telling me," she says. All summer everything has been wrong. She misses the hot Texas July. London is cold, and the food is expensive, and she doesn't understand the paintings or the ancient churches that I love. We never could have afforded this trip on our own, but we have generous relatives who paid for our flights, and we have budgeted down to the last penny. This trip is an opportunity, a privilege.

She tells me she wants to stay in tonight and call her boyfriend. She wants to tell him about the pigeons. He won't believe it, she says. They have never been apart so long before. I thought I would have my sister to myself this summer, that we would be as inseparable as we were when we were children, but he has her just as much as he ever did. They have been dating too long, and I do not like him, one more thing I may not be able to protect her from.

"Call him if you want," I say. "I'm going out."

When we were young we wished upon things that could fly—swallows and fireflies and dandelions floating through the air. I read to my sister from storybooks. We read about evil stepmothers and pirate ships and fairies. Our father could be angry and violent, and our mother was too sad about something I didn't understand to stand up to him, so we read about Peter Pan and Wendy and her brothers, and I told my sister that she was my shadow, stitched to me with thread that would not break, and I would always look after her. She seemed like a bird to me then, bright and colorful and loud, a goldfinch maybe, or an oriole. She sang in a voice that made people turn and listen, and when she walked into a room everyone dropped what they were doing and rushed to be with her. But they didn't see her when the crowds left, when we were back at home and she stopped singing. Only I saw her then.

Alone in the city I feel free enough to run, maybe even to fly. Cleaning crews have already bagged most of the bodies, all but the ones floating in the water. A few scattered feathers fly in the wind, and spots of white stain the pavement. Yesterday my sister and I went to Mass at St. Paul's Cathedral, listened to the children's voices echoing in the domes, stepped outside to flocks of pigeons waiting to be fed. That was yesterday, though, and today the pigeons are gone, and London feels louder than it did before. I miss the flapping wings and coos that softened motors and horns.

In Kensington Gardens I pass an older couple sitting on a bench near the pond. "I don't understand it," the woman cries. She carries a loaf of bread, her daily routine. Her husband rubs her back and tries to soothe her. He tells her don't worry, they will be back, more pigeons will be born next year and will be just as pesky as they ever were, but the bodies blanket the pond, and it is hard to believe his prediction.

"Do you know what happened?" I ask, and the man shakes his head.

I want him to give me some reason, something scientific and understandable, but all he says is that the world is changing. "It's not the same place it was when I was a boy."

"Yes, but in one night?" I say.

"If you ask me, something was wrong before last night," he says. "Something has been wrong for a long time."

The woman offers me some bread. I accept it and tear bites off while I walk through the gardens. I stop by the statue of Peter Pan and remember reading to my sister. When I was a child, I pretended to enter the story and scold Peter Pan for being so selfish. I'd always loved the first line, though. "All children, except one, grow up." Once I thought that fairies danced in the forest after dark, that clouds were the beds that angels slept on, that the raindrops that fell in the Texas storms each summer were holy tears from the gods. I don't believe those things anymore.

Beneath the statue is the body of a pigeon that the cleaning crew missed. I crouch down to it and touch its feathers, the dark gray stripes on the wings, the flash of green on the neck. I feel its talons that are so sharp but that never scratched the children who came to the park to chase the birds. I wonder where this one flew, what sights it saw—the London Eye or Big Ben, young brides in wedding dresses, mothers pushing strollers, through a window a dark bedroom, a fist, a belt. I scoop it up and dump it in the trash.

I haven't told my sister yet about the missed period and the cells forming inside me, no larger yet than one of the plastic beads we used to string into matching necklaces when we were children, haven't even decided if I'll let them become anything more. I only discovered them a few days ago, and I'm too young, not ready, not in love. My sister would be happy, though. She has always wanted little brothers or sisters and would love to be an aunt. She doesn't know yet the weight of that kind of love, how it must always guard and protect and sacrifice and save.

When I return that night my sister is already asleep. I dream that the pigeons return to life, as large as eagles. They fly every child away to Never Never Land, where Peter Pan explains his decision to stay, says that if he never grows up then he will never hear his father's voice echoed in his own.

I come from a family of lost boys. It stretches back further than I can remember, back to my great grandfather, who rode the orphan trains out west to a family who overworked and starved him. Back to my grandmother, who fled from Germany before WWII, lived her whole life guilty that she had survived while her cousins hadn't. Back to her husband, an angry Irishman who touched his daughters in places they shouldn't have been touched, who chased my father with a baseball bat. Back to my parents, the anger that boils right below the surface. I have fought my whole life to protect my sister, to keep her from becoming another one of our lost boys. But now there is another generation inside of me, and I wonder what transformation people undergo when they become parents. Does it rearrange their cells, remodel their bones, stitch their nerves and tendons together in new and unpredictable ways? What is it in having a child that makes a good person turn violent? What curse will I pass down? I do not want to find out.

My sister and I buy food to picnic in Hyde Park. She loves that she is old enough to drink here and wants to bring wine, but I find an excuse, just in case. The park is almost empty. Most people are not ready to talk about the pigeons, and so they stay in their homes and cars. The ones who have ventured out are full of ideas, overly simplistic ideas to make this less frightening than it should be. This has happened before, they say, a dozen or so birds falling dead out of the sky, only now it's more extreme; the weather is so much warmer this summer, and the pigeons haven't had time to adapt; there's always been talk of population control, so maybe someone tried it over-successfully.

My sister and I find a place to sit. We tear bread and make sandwiches out of cheese and salami, and the sun is shining this afternoon, and we laugh and talk.

"How's Stuart?" she asks me.

"Oh, you know," I say, and she shakes her head at me, because she does know, better than anyone else, at least, the way I'll discard him when the summer is over, ignore his calls for the next few months, then find someone new.

"And how about your guy?" I ask. "What's his name? Ben? Jason?"

She throws a chunk of bread at me. "Funny," she says. "He's good. I miss him."

"I gathered," I say. Her inability to be away from him is as confusing to me as my inability to love my boyfriends is to her. "I've never met two sisters so unalike," we hear often.

Geese wander the park. They avoid the water as much as possible, now that it is filled with bodies. My sister and I throw bread and they race each other to get to it first. "Did you know that pigeons remember humans who are kind to them?" my sister says. "I read it once. And they mate for life and raise their children together. That's why you never see baby pigeons, even though the adults are everywhere. Because their parents take such good care of them that they stay hidden until they are safely grown."

Soon we are remembering, the way we often do when we are alone.

"Do you remember when we wrote that Christmas play for our parents?"

"Do you remember when our father took us camping and swam with us under the icy waterfall?"

"Do you remember the time we first rode our bikes to the store alone?"

There are things we do not say.

I do not say, "Do you remember the time you broke the window and our father turned your body purple with bruises?"

My sister does not say, "Do you remember when our mother forgot to smile for an entire summer?"

I do not say, "I am growing a baby that will have our mother's hairline and our father's nose. I am becoming our parents and this baby is becoming us, and now you too will have someone to protect."

I've taken to walking the streets alone every morning. I leave before my sister is awake, before she can ask me to stay in the hotel room with her. I visit the cathedrals and bookstores that bore her, and now that the pigeons are gone, I look for meaning in their absence, look for some way that I am to blame, the way I have looked for it my whole life. The pigeons have died, I tell myself, because once when I was thirteen I brought home all A's while my sister brought home C's, and I didn't try to defend her. Because in high school I was thin and she wasn't, although she played every sport and I only read. Because once I tried to stand between her and my father when he was angry and he knocked me over and I never tried again. Because no matter how hard I try to change, I care more about protecting myself than protecting the people who need it most, and so how on earth can my body be growing a baby?

One morning Stuart joins me in my morning walk. We have been spending less and less time together since I discovered the pregnancy. I don't want him involved in this decision, don't want to see what he turns into if he ever learns that I have made him a father. We find a pub serving breakfast and order bacon and eggs and beans. If he notices that I am eating more than I did before, he doesn't say. I ask him about his parents, what his father is like, his mother, and he shrugs the question away and tells me they are like all parents. He wants to talk about our future.

"Soon you'll be leaving," he says.

"Yes. Two more days."

"I'll call you every morning," he says. "And let's buy a ticket for you to visit soon. You'd love London at Christmastime."

I tell him that sounds nice but let's just wait and see. "We'll figure it out," I tell him. "Let's not force things."

"I wouldn't call making a plan for our relationship surviving long distance forcing things," he says, and I say my life is about to change, I'll be looking for a job, applying to grad school, moving into my own apartment, becoming a self-supporting adult. I can't promise anything.

"Are you breaking up with me?" he asks, and I wasn't planning on making it official, but this way is more humane in the long run.

"I guess I am."

On our last night in London, my sister and I feel nostalgic. Whatever closeness we have here will be gone when we fly back home, when she goes off to college and navigates her first few months living alone, when I make the final decision on what I want my life to be. We pack our suitcases and ready our passports. We stuff souvenirs into pockets and plan which gifts we will give to which family members. We leave out our best dresses, some jewelry, a curling iron. We have budgeted for this night, planned to eat dinner at a restaurant instead of our hotel, planned to live extravagantly and enjoy London and each other before our plane takes us back.

The pigeons have not returned. The world outside of London is beginning to notice. People are slow to recognize when something is wrong, or slow to admit it, at least. But now the city has filled with reporters and environmentalists, and everyone has opinions and solutions. Everyone knows, or has an idea at least, what tipped the world off balance, what threw it into disorder.

We pick an Indian restaurant and order curry and chicken. We even buy a bottle of wine. I only take a few sips, but I pour glass after glass for my sister. We talk about our summer, our favorite moments. We remember the train ride to Venice in the crowded car, and our first time climbing the Eiffel Tower and punting down the River Cam. "I'm glad we got this summer together," I say.

We talk about the next year, too, how everything is about to change for both of us. We talk about the friends she hopes to make at college, the grad school applications I'm working on. "Not for me," she says about grad school, which I know already. We are very different, my sister and I. I think about telling her about the baby, this last night before we return home to school and family, to ask her what she thinks I should do, but the words don't come out, and I cannot make them.

After dinner, I say, "Come on, let's do something."

"Let's go home," my sister says, but I don't want our trip to end yet. I tell her I want to do one last fun thing and ask her where she wants to go, but she only wants to go back to the hotel.

"Let's see what St. Paul's looks like at night," I suggest.

"No thanks," says my sister.

I say it could be beautiful, it could be the most beautiful thing in the world and we would have missed it.

"I don't really care," says my sister. She says she'd rather go home and call her boyfriend, just to make sure he'll be meeting us at the airport, and right then I am so tired, tired of changing my plans and sacrificing and being the oldest. I never asked to be an older sister, never even asked to be a daughter. I think of Peter Pan refusing to go back to London with Wendy, and I understand him now.

"You can do what you want, but I'm going to St. Paul's," I say. My sister says she can't walk home alone, it's too late, and she's afraid. I shrug and say, "Then stay with me."

"That's not fair," she says. I know she will give in, she wouldn't know what to do without me. But she stares for a moment and says, "I'll see you at the hotel," and then walks away.

I should chase after her, at least to remind her to be careful, to take the busiest route back and keep her passport hidden, or maybe to apologize and say we've had a good trip, let's just go back together, but I don't.

St. Paul's at night is enchanted. I stand on the steps and look up and up and up, and the cathedral feels taller in the darkness, older, closer to something ancient and mystical. The rain begins to fall, a light drizzle through the streetlights, and the towers shine, and the spires pierce the night sky, and the saints seem to ascend to heaven.

When I return to the hotel, I will tell my sister what she missed, the way I stood in front of St. Paul's in the rain and felt like I was standing in the clouds, and how all the heaviness lifted and I felt sure of what I wanted. I will tell her that there in the rain with the water splashing on the pavement and my hair curling in the humidity, I felt strong enough to have the baby and protect it for the rest of my life.

My sister is curled up tight back at the hotel. Her shoulders shake, and I see she is crying. I kneel next to her. "What's wrong?" I say. "What happened?"

"You should have come with me." She gulps at the words between sobs and I sit on the bed and rub her back. I slip easily into this role.

"Tell me what happened," I say.

"I forgot which way to go. I thought the path would lead to the street but it didn't."

"You got lost?" I ask. My voice is soft and gentle, and I pour her a glass of water. I was selfish back at the restaurant and shouldn't have left her alone, but now I am here again, and I know how to comfort her. "I'm sorry, baby sister."

"Not just lost," she says. "There were these boys and they followed me and I began running but they ran even faster." She tells me how the path ended in a locked gate. "I was cornered," she says, and she looks at me like she thinks I could have unlocked the gate. "They started grabbing at me." She sits up now and shows me where they tore her shirt. Her skin is scratched, and she has bruises on her arm. She looks small, only a little girl.

All children grow up, begins *Peter Pan*. They soon know they will grow up.

"I'm so sorry," I whisper, and I'm afraid, not just for her, but also for me, because I know whatever happens next, it will be my fault, mine to live with forever.

She tells me that she didn't know what to do, stuck between the boys and the locked gate, and she felt helpless. But then she realized she could slip through the bars that were too narrow for them to fit through and run away.

So that's all, I think. The boys were surely only teasing her. If they really wanted to, they could have done much worse than tear her shirt.

I want to brush it off, tell her at least nothing happened, we shouldn't make a big deal of this and let it discolor our whole trip. But she looks at me, and I can see she is terrified, and I know I am to blame, because while I was watching the rain fall on the church at midnight, she was lost and afraid and alone.

"This is why we were supposed to stay together," she says.

"I am so, so sorry."

"All you cared about was seeing that stupid church again," she says.

All across London the pigeons have died, gentle birds who raise their young together and remember human kindness, and somehow I feel to blame. And back when we were children, I had the better table manners and made the better grades and did everything right, and I've felt guilty about it my whole life. But I can't anymore.

"It's not my fault," I say. "It hasn't ever been my fault."

"So then it's mine?" she asks.

"It's nobody's." I say it's not hers and it's not mine and it's not our father's or our mother's. It's the Second World War, and turn-of-the-century orphan care, and it's the Potato Famine in Ireland, and the tornado that ripped through Texas that one hot spring day. And it's how Columbus met indigenous people with violence and slavery, and maybe it's how his father treated him, and it's fear, and desperation, and Eve giving the apple to Adam even when she knew it would kill him, and we sit on our hotel bed and feel it all, the weight of all the history we're supposed to push against.

"Come with me," I say, and she follows.

We make our way to the Thames. It glows silver under the lamplight. It is long past midnight. Dark shadows of pigeons that have not yet been cleaned out float through the water.

"Let's save them," I say. "As many as we can." They are soggy and rotting in the water.

"That's disgusting," she says.

"I know, but let's do it anyway."

"You're insane," my sister says, but she is starting to smile, and I know that the idea is pulling her in.

We find an empty box to scoop birds out of the river. I go first. I lean down and dip the box into the cluster of bodies. I fish two out of the river and raise the box for my sister to see. "Let's name them Rosalind and Orlando" I say, "after Shakespeare, because we are in London," and I give a eulogy for them before I dump them in the nearest trashcan.

It's my sister's turn now. She laughs, loud and nervous. She pulls just one bird from the river. "Genevieve," she names it. "You lived a good and full life and died before your time," she says, and she lays the bird to rest. All night we take turns, scooping bodies, naming them, giving them stories. "This one is Pedro. He was in love with a lady pigeon once, but they were separated in a rain storm and never found each other." "Here is Angela. She dreamed of flying to the countryside, far away from the smog and noise." "Alexander loved the children in Hyde Park. He hoped for a family of his own one day." We begin pairing the pigeons up, putting them in families, brothers and sisters and mothers and fathers. We give them lives that they would want to escape. Our game is no longer fun, but we cannot seem to stop, a daughter pigeon who wants to fly away but cannot, a baby pigeon with a broken leg that needs care, a mother pigeon who is afraid of her husband. We are not laughing anymore.

"This one is her father's favorite," I say. "But she doesn't want to be. She would give her little sister everything if she could."

"This one would give her sister everything too," my sister says. "She always would have, even though her sister never saw it."

She doesn't have to say anything else then, because I remember. I remember how when we were children she'd rescue my stuffed animals for me when they fell off my top bunk and I worried for their safety, how she was always there to hold my hand and dry my eyes after our father was violent, how she filled the house with laughter and singing when our mother couldn't, how on days when the pressure of making the highest grades wore on me she bought me coffee even though she couldn't afford it.

I wonder then if love does not trickle down, from parent to child, from big sister to little, but maybe works in reverse, the younger saving the older, the grandchild redeeming the grandfather, the weaker protecting the strong.

I pick up another pigeon. "This one is pregnant and doesn't really want to be, and she has no idea what to do or what type of mother she'll be, and she is so scared. She wants to tell her sister, but she doesn't know how."

My sister is ready with another pigeon, but she drops it now. She comes over to me, and sits down beside me, and she puts her hand on top of mine.

It's almost dawn, the sky gray and bright. Overhead a flock of birds fly, starlings, black against the heavens. They clatter and screech at the new day. The sun begins to rise, and the light seems to sing, and far away in the east a few clouds glow with the pale pink of morning.

CREDITS

The following stories have appeared, sometimes with slightly altered titles or content, in these journals:

"Kansas Before Oz" in *Mid-American Review*
"Statues" in *Monkeybicycle*
"Carnival Ride" in *Word Riot*
"Día de Gracias" in *Washington Square Review*
"Donation" in *Booth*
"Astromorphosis" in *Waxwing*
"Snow Globe" in *The Adroit Journal*
"Aerial Spray" in *r.kv.r.y. quarterly*
"Frontera Seca" in *CutBank*
"Volcano Climber" in *Juked*
"'Til Morning" in *The Pinch*

ACKNOWLEDGEMENTS

Thank you to all who made this book possible:

To my teachers and mentors at the University of North Texas: Miroslav Penkov, Dr. Barbara Rodman, Dr. John Tait, and Dr. Javier Rodriguez.

To the writers and colleagues who read and shaped these stories: Andy Briseño, Sidney Thompson, April Murphy, Justin Bigos, Caitlin Pryor, Shannon Sawyer, Andrew Tolle, Marykate Messimer, and especially Erin Stalcup, Zach VandeZande, and Elise Matthews, for reading multiple drafts of each story to help it find its truest self.

To the Colegio Americano crew, for giving me so many ideas, cheering me on, and double-checking my Spanish: Shannon Hickey de Alverez, Caitlin McHugh Lenguas, Kristen Erickson Martinez, Lenya Bloom, Sarah-Eve Philippe-Beauchamp, Nicola Dorothy McDermott Cantu, Cynthia García De León, Claritza Rodríguez, Kendra Dixon, Corie Hooker, Brittany Fernández, Sarah Fedoruk, and Jenn Burkhead.

To Jenny McConnell and Lindsey Panxhi, for a lifetime of reading and dreaming together.

To Ashley Reis, for the duplex days writing the dissertations that would become our first books.

To my grandparents, Bob and Mary Fran Conley, for giving me the magic of the northwest as a child, for loving and supporting me and setting me up to do the things I wanted to do with my life.

To my aunt, Jeanne Conley, for giving me my first journal on my tenth birthday, where I wrote my first stories, for making me believe writing a book was possible.

To my father, Mark Craggett, for his humor and pride, and to my mother, Jacquie Craggett, for her everlasting support and her courage to let me be the person I need to be.

To my first sisters, Cara and Kelsey and Kylee, my longest and best teammates. And to my littlest siblings, Nathan and William and Caitlin and Kaila. You are my reason.

Photo: Caprock Studios

Courtney Craggett's short stories appears in *The Pinch, Mid-American Review, Washington Square Review, CutBank,* and *Booth,* among others. Her reviews appear in *American Microreviews and Interviews.* She holds a PhD in creative writing and Mexican-American literature from the University of North Texas, where she served as the fiction editor for *American Literary Review.* She is an assistant professor of English at Weber State University.